# RANSOM...

The long thin blade of a switch knife pointed a shining steel finger at Iris. The man turned to Lunsford. "How about it, lover boy, is it a trade? You get the girl. We get the dough."

# RUN FOR THE MONEY

by
Robert Colby

**WILDSIDE PRESS**

www.wildsidepress.com

Copyright © 1960 by Robert Colby

# CHAPTER ONE

THE ARMORED CAR rolled south on Route One out of Jacksonville, passed the last of the motels on the outskirts and slid into open country. Seven tons of steel plating and bulletproof glass. Three guards within, two in the cab and another behind the steel partition with the money sacks. Each guard carrying a .38 police special in his holster. A police riot gun bracketed on the wall of the rear compartment.

A fortress on wheels.

It was a Thursday morning, just after nine o'clock, and the sun was already beginning to sear the landscape. It was going to be the hottest October day on record in Florida. The interior of the sealed truck was warm, though not unpleasantly so, since the big ducts were scooping in a good circulation of air. The company had threatened to install air conditioning, but so far it was only a threat.

The truck was scheduled to run south for something like a hundred miles, depositing sums of money at banks in cities and towns along the way. To replenish their dwindling supply, the banks had ordered cash from the nearest source—the Federal Reserve in Jacksonville. Nothing unusual. A standard procedure. The trucks hauled cash from the Federal Reserve Bank every week.

The guard behind the partition, Wally Trautman, was sitting in the company of nine hundred sixty thousand dollars, not including the great sacks of change. He did not look at the sacks. Or think of the green power of nearly a million dollars at his finger tips. The money did not belong to him, would never be his. It was so much paper and coin. It was The Job.

Nor did he think of the possibility that the money might be stolen in a holdup. When friends offered crackpot theories on how this could be accomplished, he would just smile enigmatically. Or chuckle derisively. He knew it couldn't be done and, too, all the reasons why the best of pros wouldn't be stupid enough to try it. The safeguards he and the others performed were mechanical—just part of The Job.

No, Wally did not think of the money's buying power or its improbable loss. Instead, as the truck rumbled south, he thought of his twenty-three-year-old wife, who was seven months into her first pregnancy and still much too active in spite of his pleading. She did all the washing and mending and ironing and cleaning and marketing, carrying the baby around with her as though it were just a few pounds of added weight that would, in a couple of months, be lost in a single day. Wally was secretly proud of his wife's continued fidelity to the details of housekeeping. And grateful, too. But openly he made an incessant fuss about it. And because his wife only smiled and promised but paid no attention to him, and because he loved her as few loved their wives, he decided at this moment that when he got home he was going to positively *order* her to cut out the heavier work—and no back talk.

Up front, the driver, Pete Quillen, yawned hugely and the guard beside him, Joe Tiriolo, gave light to a cigarette and puffed silently. Quillen was thinking about his bad luck in losing a new girl friend to the higher rewards of stenography in the North, wondering whether as sweet and willing a dish would be apt to come along any time in the near future. Tiriolo had been out late and was still sleepy. He thought of nothing and wished for nothing—except to be in the sack.

A quarter mile behind, the police cruiser eased along at about the same speed as the truck. There were two officers on the front seat, and they were watchful of the road ahead. The police radio crackled and a voice droned routine business of the hour.

The officer beside the driver said, "Well . . . whattaya think, Chet?"

"Traffic's dead right now," answered Chet in a tight voice. "Might as well deliver the bad news."

"Yeah," said the other. "Might as well. Jesus God,

I hope . . . Go ahead then, Chet. Christ, let's get it over with."

The officer called Chet stepped down on the accelerator, got the red blinker on and hit the siren. Highway flew beneath the wheels, and the squat rear of the armored car grew upon them. They swerved around it, slowed and drew abreast.

They could see Pete Quillen looking down at them from his driver's perch behind the bulletproof glass with some small alarm. Frantically, they waved him over to the side of the road and, when he had stopped the truck, pulled the squad car up just in front on the shoulder.

Chet cut the blinker and hopped out, the other cop behind him. They were both lean, tall and militant in their uniforms. Chet came up to the cab, and Quillen called through the window, "Hiya, Chet! What the hell's the matter?"

"Got some bad news, Pete," Chet answered in a dejected voice. "One of your boys—"

"What? Can't hear ya, Chet!" Quillen opened the door.

"I said, just got some bad news for one of your boys, Pete. You got a guy name of Wally Trautman aboard?"

"Trautman? Sure thing. He's in back. What's the trouble?"

"His wife was just in a hit-run, crossing the street from a supermarket. They took her to the hospital. Bad shape." He leaned in and lowered his voice. "Dying," he said confidentially.

"God almighty," said Quillen, frowning deeply. "Good God almighty!"

"We'll take Trautman back with us," said Chet. "Then we'll get the company to send you out a relief man, pronto. Meantime you can move along, and they'll catch up with you before Augustine."

"Well, I dunno," answered Quillen.

"Better tell Trautman," the officer called Chet said, as his partner next to him listened and watched with a drawn face.

"Right," answered Quillen.

But Trautman had heard some part of it, leaning close behind the glass. Suddenly he slid the heavy connecting steel door back in the partition and crouched his way into the cab.

"My wife!" he shouted. "You talking about my wi—"

That was when the police officer whose name was Chet came up fast with the .38 from his holster and shot Trautman twice through the chest. Trautman collapsed with a look of utter disbelief growing and then fading across his features.

The other officer shot Quillen through the head at almost the same time and caught Tiriolo in the side and neck before Tiriolo could get his own weapon all the way out of the holster.

Then Chet shoved the body of the driver, Quillen, aside onto the floor. At which point a third man, who had been hiding in back of the police car, approached wearing a guard's cap and gloves. He hopped in the cab, slammed the door and drove off as the other two regained the police cruiser.

It had taken just over a minute, and now the first car after the traffic lull was just coming into distant view from the south.

## CHAPTER TWO

THE POLICE CAR moved quickly ahead of the armored truck, and, when the tourist with the Pennsylvania license passed in the other direction, Chet said, "Out-of-state. He'll be home before he reads about it. Eh, Buck?"

"Yeah. The whole thing went like a clock."

"So far," said Chet. "So far. Don't foul up the rest."

Buck didn't answer. He had climbed in back and was changing into slacks and a sport shirt. He put the uniform, gun and belt in a shopping bag. "Ready," he said. "Pass the iron."

Chet removed the .38 from his holster and handed it over. It went into the shopping bag with the uniform. Chet got his unused service weapon from the glove compartment and holstered it.

Now a car passed from the north and faded away. The truck was far behind. Another quarter mile and Chet stopped the cruiser at a tree-lined dirt road running off to the right. Carrying the sack with its uniform and weapons, Buck hopped out.

"Make it fast," said Chet. "Fast! I gotta get back into my territory before they miss me. Unload and beat it. And don't leave so much as a butt around there." He squinted ahead. "Car coming from the south. Shove. Run! Tonight at seven."

Buck moved off at a fast trot and lost himself in the trees. Chet was already hurling the police car back toward town. As he passed the truck he grinned broadly and gave a big salute.

In a small clearing among the trees off the dirt road, Buck hauled the tarpaulin from the Ford sedan. The tarp was the speckled camouflage type used by the army for concealment from spotter planes. He got the motor going, then opened the trunk. After the armored car had pulled alongside, the fake driver opened the package door from inside and began feeding the money sacks to Buck. When the trunk was loaded and locked, they checked the bodies in the bloody cab. Trautman, Tiriolo and Quillen were all dead.

Now they covered the truck with the big tarp, removed their gloves and drove off in the Ford. "You forget something, Perry?" said Buck as they approached the highway.

"Forget? What you mean?"

"Try your head."

"Oh," said Perry, snatching off the guard cap. "Oh, Jesus."

"Now get out and check if anything's coming," said Buck, stopping the car.

Perry walked to the edge of the highway and looked in both directions. Then he signaled and, when the Ford came abreast of him, jumped in. They moved slowly in the direction of Jacksonville.

"Now all we gotta do is lay now and wait," said Buck.

"Yeah," said Perry. "Just read the papers."

## CHAPTER THREE

A MONTH LATER, on a Monday morning in November, Barry Lunsford was driving east from Tampa on Route 84. He was going to connect with Route One, which would take him to Miami.

Up ahead he could see the gate swing closed at the railroad crossing. There was the distant clang of the warning bell, and in a moment what seemed half a mile of freight train lumbered down the track. A trio of cars were braked to a stop, and he pulled in behind them and cut the motor.

Mentally he groaned. The caboose wasn't even in sight, and he could run faster than that freight was moving. Why couldn't it have been one of those silver streamliners that swirl by in a matter of seconds?

Lunsford had been visiting an army buddy, like himself a bachelor, in Tampa. His friend had a small apartment but a large address book. It had been one of those weekends you could dissolve with nothing less than a gallon of water and ten hours sleep.

He could get the water all right. But eight hours of clerking in a department store on Biscayne Boulevard separated him from sleep. It was a sixty-a-week job, strictly a stopgap necessity. He hated it. And the scarred little sweatbox of a furnished room off 79th. And the grubby hamburger joints, the four-bit movies and the faltering forty-nine Chevy he was driving.

Perversely, with only a half dozen cars to wheel beyond the crossing, the freight thundered and squealed to a complete halt. Lunsford looked at his watch. Seven-twenty-eight. Time enough to shave and shower—if the bath down the hall wasn't jammed with fellow roomers—grab the thirty-five-cent special at Royal Castle and head for work.

Yawning, he got out of the car and stretched. He walked around front and, leaning against the right fender, fired a cigarette. The narrow road climbed slightly before it thumped over the tracks. There were a few feet of shoulder, then a steep embankment. As he thought idly of the ease with which a sleepy or careless driver could tumble over, he heard the motor die in the car ahead. Just catching on, buddy? That new Olds gobbles high-test at ·thirty-four and nine a gallon, you know. The driver, a big guy in a short-sleeved mustard sport shirt, looked sullen and groggy. Lunsford watched him unfold a newspaper across the wheel and wondered where he was going and how he made a buck.

The sun was setting up for a bright day. Warm but pleasant. A few widely spaced cloud puffs drifting white and friendly. A moist bite to the air. He thought of fishing. And the beach with its tawny-legged girls, paunchy men from the north, with cushy jobs, watching them. And in the afternoon, the money-maw of the race track swallowing the easy dollars. And the giant hotels with the flunkies to serve the rich at play.

Then he saw the railroad brakeman in the blue denims and peak cap signal from the caboose. For a moment the train backed, then moved slowly forward. He read the names on the cars and watched the wheels grind track. His eyes slid down from the apex where track bed and road embankment met. Below were tin cans, a litter of paper and . . . something else. Something of dark blue canvas with brown leather trim. Some kind of carrying case, because it had a handle. Whatever it was, it was incongruous in that rubble. Not a thing to be tossed away. New-looking.

Lunsford knew that moment of indecision most people have when they spot something discarded or lost, but distant and awkwardly accessible. And he thought, Aw hell, if it was worth anything, it wouldn't be there. Nothing is for nothing in this world. Close up, the case would be broken or torn. And there was that small blow to his pride—to think that he would take the time and trouble to scavenge around in refuse. Suppose someone saw him?

So he waited until the last freight car had rumbled past, the gate had opened and the autos had gone. Then he drove the car to a point just above the spot and off the road. Taking the keys, he descended, gathering dirt in his shoes and on his trouser cuffs, feeling ridiculous and a little ashamed.

He saw right away that it was one of those clothes carriers—a two-suiter. Made of canvas and leather, folded and fastened for carrying. He picked it up, and it was heavy enough. One side was dirty, but otherwise it was in excellent shape. He pulled the zipper on its half-moon track and peered inside cautiously, expecting anything, including parts of a body.

But what it contained was money. A great green flurry of it choking the interior. Several bills floated out, and he caught them in a mad scramble, shoving them back inside, closing the case. He looked above him nervously. There were no cars, so he hauled himself up the embankment, opened the trunk, tossed the case and closed the lid.

Then he did see a car approaching behind him. Quickly, he ducked and began an inspection of one of the tires.

He heard the car slow. But when he looked up it was only a girl in a black Ford. She wasn't going to stop, just braking for the crossing, giving him no more than a curious glance as she passed.

Behind her was a station wagon, but before it reached him he had climbed in and pulled out of there, trying not to hurry. Trying to keep his excitement from communicating itself to the gas pedal.

He had gone only a short distance when, just ahead, he saw a line of cars piled up, single file. The cars moved forward at a crawl. Soon he understood why. Two patrol cars were stationed at either side of the road, and two officers were checking cars passing in both directions.

A feeling of panic overcame him. He had an unreasonable sense of guilt—almost as though he were escaping after the commission of a crime. He knew that, in essence, this was the sort of fear experienced by the criminal at the sight of every cop. Yet, what had he done? Was it a felony to find money? In a two-suiter without a single identification?

The guilt was not in finding money. But so *much* money. In such quantity, found money was full of implications—all of them trouble.

He looked behind him. Backing up was impossible. The following car was all but leaning on his bumper. And behind that one, three more. When the line moved forward, he thought of making a quick turn-around. But he would be seen, and it would look suspicious. What the hell. If the money was the tail end of a crime, he didn't want it, anyway. Did he. . . ? The first sight of it had moved him to a driving, hungry sense of possession. New currents of thought had begun to drift through his mind.

Now Lunsford saw that the policemen were not only peering with slow careful eyes into the cars, but also examining drivers' licenses. The car ahead was allowed to pass. He came to a halt before the officer. A big hand fell lazily upon the door, the sun touching a plain gold ring on the officer's little finger. Around the ring, small blond hairs curled.

Lunsford's eyes fell upon the service revolver holstered at the officer's side. The gun seemed a threat.

The cop's face was placid as his eyes roved the interior and came back to Lunsford.

"See your license please, sir?" Nothing in the voice at all but a polite demand.

"Sure thing," he said, and got the paper from his wallet with awkward fingers and too much show of haste. The cop appeared not to notice his nervousness as he inspected the license and handed it back.

"Now your registration please, sir." His tone had become a little bored.

"What's it all about, officer?" he asked as he produced the ownership paper.

The officer didn't answer until he had looked over the registration and returned it.

"Nothing much," he said. "Routine inspection. We have them about every month now, one place or another."

"What do you look for?"

"People who forget to renew their operator's license. Or don't have one at all. Especially them. Vehicles with improper registration. Or none."

"Catch a lot of 'em, eh?"

"You'd be surprised. You'd just be surprised. Move along, please, sir."

## CHAPTER FOUR

BEHIND THE locked door of his room, Lunsford set the blue case on the bed and stared at it. With a feeling of unreality. And with awe. For he knew that case contained his future.

But for a moment he hesitated. He hadn't really examined the bills, and he was afraid it was going to be a very bad joke, that it would be stage money, or at least counterfeit. Then he reached down suddenly, hauled the zipper around its track and pulled back the flap.

He grabbed the first bill that came under his hand and examined it in the light. It was a twenty, and it wasn't stage money. It was an old bill, and had the unmistakable look and feel of genuine Uncle Sam printing. Nevertheless, he gave it a few standard tests that erased all doubts. He did the same with several other loose bills, then dumped the entire contents on the bed.

Most of the bills were in stacks and tied with pieces of thin white string. It was obvious what had happened. The case had either fallen or been tossed from above, and two of the stacks had spewed loose bills when it struck. He tried to picture the case falling from some vehicle or a careless hand. But, looking at the green welter, he couldn't make himself read carelessness into the loss. Not carelessness, not even drunkenness. Only a lunatic would let that kind of cash get out of hand for a single moment.

There were of course, freak accidents, even with money. And that was one possibility. He tried for another.

An express train with its coach, baggage and pullman cars hurtling through the night, its deep plaintive voice like some great agonized beast, crying a warning to the crossing. And, in a rocking car of the train, a window or a door open, the case flung at a precise moment for some unimaginable reason. Or falling by some still more unimaginable accident.

Or take the same line of thought and place the money in a passing auto.

Finally, picture someone on foot using that unlikely spot as a place of hiding. Ridiculous!

Yet it had to be one of these. Because he wasn't even going to consider a plane. Or should he? In any case, why? Why, why, why?

One thing seemed quite certain. The money had not been there long. An hour or two, several at the most. The attendant of an all-night gas station down the road had told him it had rained buckets during the night, and the case showed no signs of weathering.

In a few minutes he gave up speculating in favor of the count. Most of the bills were fifties and hundreds. As he made the count, he did an occasional spot check, but there were no phonies. Because most of the bills were in five-thousand stacks, it didn't take long.

Lunsford figured it right at three hundred twenty thousand dollars.

It was too much money to comprehend all at once, to put in terms of living and spending. He could think in terms of hundreds. And his imagination stretched to the banking of a couple of thousand in a savings account after a heroic two years of sweating twenty bucks off the top of a hundred a week. But three hundred twenty thousand was something in a newspaper about the cost of a court house, or a small bridge, or the city budget for a new traffic light system. He could only sit there numbly, letting the bills drift through his fingers.

After a while, though, he found a way to make the money real. He played a little game. Salaries in Miami, except for the chosen few, were well below the scale of a city like New York or Chicago or Los Angeles. So he could hold up a fifty-dollar bill and say to himself, There's a waitress, one of the lucky ones, after a forty-eight-hour, six-day week. Six days of toting dishes on tired feet, hopping to the orders, smiling to the surly complaints, running for the little coins under the plates. And, from that fifty, don't forget to pay The Man.

And here's fifty for the bus driver's week after taxes, and all the janitors, and street cleaners and cashiers and rookie cops and office girls and clerks in a hundred stinking categories, all of them on the sweaty jump for that little fifty-dollar bill he held in his hand. The same fifty-dollar bill that was not quite his after taxes.

Now take a whole stack of fifties, a five thousand stack and hold it up. And you've got all those same tired puppets being goosed along, chasing for their rock-bottom, dirt-cheap necessities, their grubby mortgaged houses and broken mortgaged cars and third-rate furniture and meat-loaf, veal-chop meals. For how long? Roughly, two grinding heartbreaking years. For that one five-thousand stack.

And in that five-thousand stack he saw himself hustling for the same two years. And then he began to understand about the meaning of this money in front of him.

Finally he took one of the five-grand piles and told himself, Here's one of the bigger better convertibles, brand new. Or here's a first class trip to Europe. Or here's a new boat, small but sleek and fast. Or here's a five-year supply of two-hundred-dollar suits and forty-dollar shoes and twenty-dollar shirts. Or here's a full no-work year at double my salary. All for that one stack. Just one. Take three and you've got a development house.

Take them all and you've got a lifetime of freedom and luxury living.

And that was when he really understood why he couldn't let that money get out of his hands.

He was thirty-two years old, and until that moment he did not think he would ever be anything or have anything. Not even the distinction of good looks. Just an average guy of middle height with brown hair, brown eyes and unremarkable features. He did have a naturally good physique, and he kept it that way with exercise—mostly push-ups from the table. But he had always been and would always be one of the millions of anonymous drones working for somebody else and owing the bank for two-thirds of every important possession. Not that he was dumb, either. His was no giant mind, but he was a pretty intelligent guy. High school education and a couple of years of night-school college. Not for credits—just for the kick of learning. But, like ninety per cent of the world slaves, he just couldn't make out working for anyone else. Not in a big way. He couldn't move up in the system to some plateau where he ceased to merely exist and began to live in a state of comparative luxury.

He knew why. It was simple. He was fundamentally incapable of paying the price. To climb in the ordinary drab business, you had to take a gigantic interest in dry details that were a colossal bore. Or you had to pretend to. And he couldn't do either. You had to play patsy with some awful slobs who had once been puppets, too, but, having arrived, now became martinets. As though to revenge themselves upon you for the crap they had taken on the move up. You had to pretend to like these bastards and eat their exhaust until you were one of them. And then, when you were up there, you had to keep a sharp knife handy to slash the competition below and cut the ropes of the boys above while they weren't looking. He couldn't do it. The whole thing was an enormous hypocricy. He tried. But he either laughed out loud or got mad and told the wrong guy off.

It was all an act. The Big Powers were great actors. And he not only couldn't play the role, he didn't want to. He couldn't take himself that seriously. Or anyone else. So he became an individual. A nonconformist. But, like most members of the noncon fraternity, he was broke nearly all the time.

The last job he had had was in the home office of a chain department store in New York. He had been assistant to the manager of the order department, Everett Putney, a prissy, unimaginative robot. They had hated each other on sight. Putney kept crowding him, and he needled back every chance he got. Then one day Putney went on vacation and left him with an impossible stack of work—all Putney's. With his own work, it was too much for him, and Putney knew it. He fell far behind, though he stayed late every night. Waldron, the head buyer in charge of the department, made a big noise about it to Putney when he returned from vacation. Putney was ready with the answers. He said Lunsford was low and inefficient, a poor man for the job because he couldn't assume responsibility.

Waldron had called Lunsford into his office. He wouldn't listen to reason, and Lunsford told him off. Waldron gave him the ax. So he clobbered Putney, one good belt that sent him sprawling across his desk, and walked out to the tittering applause of the stenographers and the smirks of the male flunkies who hated Putney no less.

He had taken the next train to Miami, figuring if he was going to be miserable the best place to endure it was Florida. He had grabbed the first job he could get—sales clerk in a department store, men's furnishings. If you're going to be nothing, he had reasoned, you might as well be nothing while toasting yourself occasionally on a sub-tropic beach.

And now here he was, staring at three hundred twenty thousand ways to escape oblivion.

## CHAPTER FIVE

AFTER BARRY Lunsford examined the interior of the case to make sure there was no scrap of paper, no marking of identification, he put the money away and sat there thinking about it. He came to the immediate conclusion that chances were ten to one no honest citizen would be carrying around the sum of over a quarter million dollars in cash. Therefore, it was likely the money had a rather seamy background. Lunsford was also a little—just a little —ashamed to admit that he didn't care very much. The money was ignorant of its own history, didn't care who spent it and stood ready to make friends with anyone who possessed it. Life itself had not been very friendly to him, but one could be certain of these three hundred twenty thousand friends. They were a whole army of conspirators who would help provide him with the best of everything in a world of iniquities where often the best went to the least deserving. And, further, these bills were not new friends but old ones, whose serial numbers were beyond tracing.

Barry Lunsford was the sort of man who would walk back a block to return a dime too much change given him mistakenly by some harried drugstore cashier. Once, when he was thirteen, he and another kid had swiped a couple of fountain pens from a five-and-dime counter. But that had been his only experience with theft. He was among the great horde of people who had said, at one time or another, If I were going to steal, I'd take a million or nothing. But a plan for stealing a million with impunity had not been presented to him, and, anyway, it was quite possible that if one did he would have been unable to execute it, his conscience being what it was.

However, found money seemed another thing entirely. A man who found money beyond tracing and didn't spend it forthwith, and without asking more than a minimum of conscience-saving but guarded questions about it abroad, was a damn fool.

All right, perhaps the money was stolen. Lunsford was not forgetful of the armored car robbery up in Jacksonville. You hadn't been able to open a newspaper for a week without reading about it. For two days the armored car and its three guards had just disappeared from the face of the earth. It had been thought that the guards were in collusion to steal the money. But finally the truck had been found concealed in a wooded area, the guards shot dead, all the money gone except some sacks of change. There were dozens of theories of how it had been done, but not a single solid clue. Yet the amount stolen was not three hundred twenty thousand but nine hundred sixty. And, anyway, a great portion of the armored car cash was new. Lunsford couldn't discount the possibility that he held some part of the money. But there was no way even the police could prove it. And now the furor had died, and the Federal insurance company had made good the loss. Lunsford would not lose any sleep over a multi-million-dollar, government-backed insurance company. His regrets were for the families of the men killed. The cold brutality of the crime was beyond his comprehension. And there it ended.

On the other hand, by some strange freak of circumstance, the money might just be the life savings of some eccentric duck who should be in an asylum but who nevertheless was carrying the money around and had lost it—for which eventuality one had to make at least a decent effort. But, even if he found the owner, Lunsford was going to get his cut, his percentage as reward. Even ten per cent would mean that his days of frugality were over. He was going to act accordingly.

Hiding the money and locking his room, he went across the street to a drugstore. In a booth he placed four calls. The first to the Miami Police Department, the second to the Sheriff's Department of Broward County where the money had been found. Had anyone reported the loss of a two-suiter containing a "considerable" amount of money?

Negative. No such report had been made.

Next he called the railroad lost-and-found. Also negative. His relief was enormous. Anyone who could prove legal ownership of the money would have called the police immediately. The railroad office, too, if the money had been lost from a train.

Beneath his excitement there was a small stab of fear. If the money belonged to criminals, he was a hunted man. But that was a burden he could bear bravely with over a quarter million. Besides, who had a single clue to his identity? In any case, he was about to take certain steps to confuse the issue and remove himself from the scene.

The final call was to Harvey MacLaren, the section manager of men's furnishings. MacLaren was a scrawny, nervous little man in his fifties. He wanted everybody to like him but didn't know how to manage it and keep control. He was a chronic worrier, the kind who worries himself into a minor command. Someone had called him Fuss 'n' Cluck, and the name stuck. "Watch it, here comes Fuss 'n' Cluck."

"What the hell, Lunsford," he whined into the phone. "It's already twenty after nine. You know there's a sale this morning, and we need every—"

"Cut!" he said.

"What?"

"I said, cut. Save it, pal. I'm not coming in."

"Not coming in? You sick, Lunsford? Or just hung-over?"

"Listen, Harv," he said, picturing MacLaren's frown of wounded dignity. No one ever called him by his first name. "Listen, Harv, ole buddy, can't make it today. Got to hop off to New York, first plane."

"New York? New York!"

"Yeah. Just got a wire. Friend of mine has an opening for me in a textile house. Office manager. Big opportunity. Can't miss it. Got to leave right away. You wouldn't hold me back, would you, Harv?"

"Well now, I . . . Kind of a spot, you know. Short notice."

"Sorry, Harv, that's the way it is."

"Well, you go ahead, Lunsford. Uh—we'll make out."

"Think you can handle it without me, eh?"

"Pardon?"

"What about my pay?"

"I'm afraid that will take some time."

"Well, send it to my home address and they'll forward. Don't forget, Harv. Need every cent, you know." He didn't care a hoot about those few bucks now. But he had to leave the impression.

"We'll mail it out, don't worry," said MacLaren. "I'll see to it."

"Thanks, Harv. Nice working with you. Really grand."

"Good luck, Lunsford."

On his way back from the drugstore he bought a large brief case, the roomy commercial sort in which samples are carried. Before climbing to his second-floor cubicle, he stopped to give the landlady, Mrs.

Ziegler, notice that he was leaving for New York immediately.

Mrs. Ziegler was squat and rather frowzy, but very kind. She was a widow and had a son, Henry, who was nineteen. They were quite poor. Henry worked as a bus boy and couldn't afford to own a car, so Lunsford asked Mrs. Ziegler if Henry would like to have his Chevy. He explained that it was of little value, and he wouldn't need it in New York. After much protesting, she took the keys and Lunsford signed the registration in favor of Henry. It wasn't pure generosity. He wanted to leave quickly, and there was no time for dickering at some used car lot.

He told Mrs. Ziegler to hold his mail until he sent her an address.

Upstairs, he transferred the money to the brief case and dumped the two-suiter into a garbage can, covering it with papers. The brief case would stay with him on the plane. He packed his few belongings in the one big bag and he was ready.

He took a cab to the airport. On the way he stopped at his bank and withdrew the ridiculous sum of one hundred thirty dollars from his savings account.

At the terminal he did not buy a ticket to New York but to Los Angeles. He had never intended to return to New York, had wanted only to cloud his movements. He had a good friend in Los Angeles, Frank Dudley. Frank owned a commercial recording company, small but successful. Frank could introduce him around and there would be the beginning of a new life. A dream life in which he would never again have to work unless he wanted to. The glorious thought of it gave him a feeling of unbearable joy.

While he waited for the plane, Lunsford wrote half a dozen postcards, to casual friends in the area. He had no close ties. He explained nothing except that he had a job in New York and had to leave suddenly.

In less than an hour, he was boarding the plane and taking a window seat, leaning back comfortably, watching the pert behind of the blonde stewardess move up the aisle and feeling grand.

In twenty minutes, the plane had left the ground and he was looking down at the fading coastline of Miami Beach as the plane banked and held course. A great town, he thought. Money trees grow beside railroad banks. But I'll never be back. Might be some deadly snakes that would sneak back in search of that particular tree. And I'm not ready to die. Not for a long, long time, buddy boy.

"How about some coffee, sir?" said the little blonde stewardess leaning above him.

He looked up at her, and his smile was dazzling, full of the magnificence of his future.

## CHAPTER SIX

SANTA MONICA. The apartment had large rooms and was pleasantly furnished in comfortable modern. It was on the fifth floor front and cost a hundred sixty a month. No strain at all. The building was on Ocean Avenue, only a few blocks from Wilshire and easy access to Hollywood or Los Angeles.

Ocean Avenue is on the coast, but highly placed above it and set well back. Far below, the Pacific Coast Highway runs toward San Francisco north, and San Diego south. From his window, Lunsford could see wide stretches of ocean and, obliquely, the long jut seaward of the Municipal Pier, boats moored in the protective calm behind the breakwater. Across Ocean Avenue there was that narrow strip of grass and shade trees with benches called The Promenade. A miniature park.

A place of charm and quiet in which to contemplate the uses of three hundred twenty thousand dollars.

Just over two months had passed since Barry

Lunsford arrived in Los Angeles. Two months and nineteen thousand dollars gone. Four thousand for a new Pontiac convertible, a thousand for a complete new wardrobe, three thousand for a diamond ring, another thousand for rent and general expenses plus living it up a bit on the nightclub circuit. Ten thousand had been invested in a silent partnership with Frank Dudley. Dudley had used the money to buy equipment and add film production to his recording business over on La Brea, films for TV commercials and industrial takes of plant operations in the area to be used by the sales staffs hustling new business. Lunsford was to get thirty per cent of the film profits. It gave him a feeling of belonging without the necessity of working unless he wanted to. When he was ready to take an active part in the business, his share of film net would be fifty per cent. Fair enough.

The balance of the money reposed safely in a deposit box at a Santa Monica branch of the Bank of America. He told no one of its existence. Not even Dudley. Instead he explained that he was the recipient of a "small" fortune inherited at his father's death. In truth, his father had left him a very small fortune indeed. Exactly eight hundred dollars and some battered furniture.

Now the world of Barry Lunsford was spinning in a bright and cloudless sky. He had money and owned part of a business—and he was in love. The girl was Iris Howland, and she did the bookkeeping for Dudley. She was a dark redhead of twenty-seven, quietly attractive, sensible and thoroughly nice. They spent their first date with Dudley and his wife; thereafter they had been together alone almost every night. On an evening at the end of the first month they had had dinner at a seaside restaurant in Malibu. The waiter brought cocktails, they touched glasses and drank. He looked out the window to the ocean, and when he turned back he found her eyes on him with a long solemn look. "You too?" he said softly. With moist eyes she nodded slowly and gave him a tremulous smile.

When he took her back to her apartment on Sunset in The Palisades, she had invited him in and, without fanfare or hypocritical mouthings about virtue, slept with him through the night. Two weeks later he had bought her a ring and they had decided to get married in April and honeymoon in Hawaii.

He knew he would have to tell her about the money, but he kept putting it off because he thought she would be more frightened than pleased when she understood the circumstances.

During the first two weeks after his arrival in L. A., Lunsford had gone every day to a stand that sold out-of-town newspapers. He had bought the Miami Herald, and he had searched for an item in the classified section advertising the loss of the money. There had been nothing. Nor had there been a single paragraph of news that might have furnished him a clue.

Meanwhile, he never quite lost the feeling of unreality that such good luck had come to him.

Nor did he lose a certain look-over-the-shoulder uneasiness. If the money was stolen, he had an enemy. And somewhere that faceless enemy was searching for the three hundred twenty thousand.

On a night in December he broke the story to Iris Howland. It just tumbled out of him unexpectedly.

He arrived early at her apartment. They were tired of nightclubs and were going to a movie at Grauman's. Fresh from a shower, she came to the door in a robe.

"Darling, you're terribly early," she scolded.

"It's a compliment," he said. "I'm anxious."

She smiled and kissed him. Giving her a pat on the rump, he walked in and fell on the sofa.

"There's the dictionary," she said. "Start your education with A—for arrival—and by the time you get to P—for premature—I'll be ready."

"Premature arrival. Very funny," he said. "There are worse things than premature arrivals. For instance there are premature—"

"Ejections," she said.

"Thanks. But that wasn't—"

"Which is what I'm going to do to you if you don't shut up and let me get ready. All I have to do is fix my hair, polish my nails, find two stockings that match and don't have a run, and get dressed."

"Can I watch?"

"While I polish my nails? Sure."

"The getting dressed part."

"N-O."

"After all, I'm going to have to get used to it sometime."

"N-O. Exclamation point."

With a teasing smile she parted the robe just enough to reveal one leg to the knee. Then she flounced off into the bedroom.

He followed her.

She was standing before the mirrored vanity, examining a confusion of bottles. He came up behind her. He knew she heard him, but she made a pretense of extreme concentration. He reached his arms around her and, parting the robe so that he could see her nakedness in the mirror, watched the reflection of his hands creeping up until they covered her breasts.

"Let's see," she said with mock boredom. "Where did I put that new bottle of perfume, the one called Sailor's Delight?"

He turned her around, and suddenly her face was troubled. "Don't you care," she said, "that there are no more mysteries?" She had a fine mouth, delicate and sensitive, and her eyes were deep lavender. "A honeymoon in Hawaii. Will it still be exciting if you go on gobbling me up?"

"Do you play chess? I've known one game to take hours. Sometimes—"

"No, I'm serious, darling."

He held her against him. "I don't like sex mysteries," he said. "You can solve them in an hour. And sometimes they're disappointing."

"Were you . . . disappointed?"

"Have you checked your ring finger lately? And remember, old lovers are the best. Practice."

"You sound so experienced."

"Mmmmm."

"You act it, too. But I find it uh . . . helpful?"

"Mmmmm." His hands wound down her back. "Besides—" touching her head—"I like what you've got up here, too. That's the best. Really. You can't make love and sleep all the time."

She kissed him. The kiss flamed small and became a fire.

"Do we really want to go to the movies, darling?" she sighed.

"No. I don't think so. Not any more."

He was dressing, and saw it was after midnight. He had fallen asleep.

"Coffee?" Iris said.

"Sounds good."

"And a hamburger?"

"I'm starved."

"And then maybe a jelly doughnut?"

"I've always been crazy about jelly doughnuts."

"I'll fix," she said. And still wearing the robe, though she had put on a nightgown underneath, went into the kitchen. He followed.

She set some water to boil and, placing cups on the table, got a jar of coffee from the cabinet.

"I'll use this instant stuff," she said, spooning it into the cups. "I like it just as well, don't you?"

"Uh-huh. Sure." He sat down, lighting a cigarette, feeling good, relaxed. This is the way it would be when they were married. Cozy, intimate. Companionable.

She got hamburger from the refrigerator and began molding patties, cutting in particles of onion.

"Wish you could stay all night, Barry."

"Me, too."

"But you know, people begin to talk. It doesn't matter that you're engaged. That Mrs. Rupley across the hall is a nosy one."

"Yeah, she looks it. Vicarious thrill type. Why doesn't she build a life of her own? Her husband must be a goddam bore."

Iris dropped the patties into a greased pan, which she then set on the range. "Not even a bore. He's nothing. Just a big glob."

"You mean gob."

"Glob, darling, glob. He's strictly a land blubber."

"Ha! Pretty sharp for this hour."

"I won't be so sharp in about six hours, when I have to get up. What does it feel like to sleep in the morning?"

"Jealous?"

"Yes." She placed doughnuts on the table and sat down. "You bet I'm jealous. Barry?"

"What?"

"Well . . . I don't want to get too personal or sound like a nagging wife prematurely—there's that word again. But, well, I know you have an interest in Frank's business and all that. And the film end is going to do well because some of his recording customers are beginning to use him for film commercials. But aren't you going to take a more active part? I'm sure you could bring in some new accounts."

"I know. And I will in time. But I'm in no hurry."

"Don't you get bored? Don't you want to work at something? I mean, don't you feel—"

"Guilty?"

"Well..."

"No. I don't feel in the least guilty. I've been pushing for a buck all my life." He was a little annoyed, because for the first time she was probing him. "And now that I've got some dough, I'm going to coast awhile and let capital carry the load. What the hell—a buck doesn't care if you're working or not, so why should I?"

"I know, but—"

"But, nothing! Do you think ninety-nine out of a hundred of the slaves out in that stupid forty-hour grind would chew their years up with work if they didn't have to? Money, great big bunches of it, says, Do what you want to, pal. Do what you want, when you want, how you want and *if* you want. That's what money says. And I'm listening to the rustle of those sweet paper voices—both ears!"

"Now please, Barry. Don't get mad, darling. I just want to get to understand you better, not to pry." She went over and flipped the hamburgers, then sat down again. There was a small silence while she played with a spoon. "Tell me it's none of my business," she went on softly. "I've never asked you before. But we *are* going to share problems and keep no secrets. So just how many of these paper voices are rustling in your ears?"

Unsmiling, he got up, crossed the room. Leaning on a window sill, he looked out, although he saw nothing. He was tired, sick of holding the secret to himself, wanting to tell someone. He turned.

"Okay," he said. "Be the first to know. It's around three hundred thousand."

"Dollars!"

"Of course."

"Oh my God. That's—that's a fortune."

"Well, you see?"

"No wonder you weren't in a hurry to work. Your father must have been awfully rich. You inherited that much—three hundred thousand dollars?"

When he didn't answer she began to dish the hamburgers and pour water in the cups, stirring the mix into coffee. Then she sat down and waited.

It had never been necessary to tell her a direct lie, and now he couldn't do it. Something in the relationship would die. "I didn't really inherit the money," he said. "Not three hundred thousand."

"What then, Barry? What then?"

"You won't believe me. No one would."

"I'll always believe you, Barry."

Her gaze was steady, and her faint smile was kind.

"All right, then. I found the money. No, really. That's just what happened. I found it."

## CHAPTER SEVEN

WHEN HE HAD explained it all patiently, she was still incredulous.

"Fantastic," she said. "Something out of a dream."

"Sure. But of course there's a logical explanation. I don't want to hear it at the price of losing the money. I'm not *that* curious. But I'll bet it would be a dilly of a tale."

"Barry?"

"Yes."

"I really think you're making a mistake," she said evenly. "I think you should turn the money over to the police for investigation."

"I told you. I called two police departments. They had nothing on it at all."

She shook her head. "Not the same thing," she said firmly. "You ought to take the money in and present all the facts. Then you might find it would tie up with something they already know."

"I only look crazy, Iris. Don't be silly. The day I part with three hundred thousand bucks until someone proves to me it's legally theirs, I'll have myself committed. You think over a quarter of a million wouldn't tempt even the police?"

"Tempt, yes. But that's all. They'd know how to handle it, and you might even get it back."

"Nuts! Remember that Chicago kidnaping case? Six hundred thousand. The police got hold of the money after the kid was killed. What happened to it? Half of it, right around three hundred thousand, got lost somehow. One of the detectives got his mits on it. They never could prove he did, as I remember. So, God knows, he's probably spending it right now."

"Don't you want your hamburger?" said Iris. "It's getting cold."

"No. All of a sudden I'm not hungry."

"Obviously the money was stolen," said Iris. "And it's a dangerous situation." She pushed her plate away and sat back, frowning.

"Besides," said Lunsford, "all the bills are old. Can a cop third-degree old money and make it tell where it came from? So what's gained?"

"I think there's some kind of legal thing about found money, Barry." She lighted a cigarette nervously. "If you turn it over to the police, they keep it for ninety days. Then, if no one claims it, why it's yours. I read that somewhere."

"Maybe. It might work for fifty or a hundred bucks, even a thousand. But three hundred thousand? Never. Somehow they'd find a dozen reasons not to give it back to you."

"Then you're going to just keep it?"

"Show me an average guy who wouldn't."

"You're not an average guy."

"Oh yes, I am. Of course I am. I'm very goddam average when it comes to money. I have a better than average liking for it, that's all. I'm so average I've got no unusual talents that are going to make me rich. The highest I ever went was assistant to the head stooge of a department. I don't bend low enough. I don't kiss enough butts to ever make it big in this world. You think I want to grovel and beg and fawn and sweat the next thirty-five, forty years for a hundred a week? If I don't have to? Why the interest alone would bring me, three, four times that. You too, Iris. It's your life, too. Think about it. My God, you surprise me. Be practical. Be a little cynical. Don't float along on those Sunday school, church social platitudes. Christ. Oh Jesus, please use your head. This is one goddam tough world we live in. The poor slobs, the cheap labor slaves, hump for every dime.

"And a life span is just a couple of drops of time in the big vacuum. Before you can figure out where it went, it ends. And time doesn't care if you're a slave or a king—it goes right on gobbling up the years. Think about it. Think, think!"

"Barry, listen to me. Don't you think I'd like to live easy, too?"

"Well then... ?"

She mashed her cigarette out violently. "The whole thing scares me. People have been murdered for ten dollars. And you've got over a quarter million that may have belonged to—to some gangsters who would kill you to get it back."

"Sure, they would. If they knew who I was or how to reach me. But they don't."

"Another thing, Barry. It may seem right for you to keep the money since you found it. But it isn't, really. And, if you want to include me, I don't think we'd ever be happy with it."

"Crap! Moralistic crap!"

"Maybe. But I wouldn't touch a penny of it unless I knew it wasn't stolen. Unless it was legally turned over to us because the owner couldn't be found."

"I hope you know what you're saying, Iris. Because I *am* going to keep the money. And it would stand between us."

"I see."

"Do you? I don't think so." He strode out of the kitchen, through the living room. The hell with her. Plenty of dames who would jump to take her place, no questions. Never tell a woman the truth, that's all.

She caught up with him at the door. She was crying. "Don't leave, Barry. Please! We'll talk it out."

"Nothing to talk about. Call me if you change your mind, Iris."

He left.

## CHAPTER EIGHT

AT SIX ON A Wednesday evening two days later, Lunsford was sitting in the bar of a restaurant on Wilshire in Santa Monica. The place was just a few blocks from his apartment. It had Hawaiian decor—much bamboo, murals of native girls in native scenes and waitresses wearing sarongs. They served tall rum drinks with names like Impatient Virgin, Cobra's Sting, Potion for Passion and Flower of Love. They all tasted alike, and the atmosphere was fake—but dark and pleasant.

Lunsford was feeling anything but pleasant. Iris hadn't called, and he had been brooding around his apartment in the first real throes of doubt. She had opened a wedge in his conscience, and he had to keep arguing with himself to escape a sense of guilt he felt was ridiculous. Iris had made him feel that, by not turning the money over to the police, he might be covering a crime. He was dishonest, even lawless. Absurd. The kind of righteous hypocrisy they told children to scare them into robot obedience to society. And yet, Iris was neither prudish nor stupid, and she had shaken his conviction. Just enough so that he was disturbed.

So now he would sit there in that booth and he would get a little drunk, just a little. And then, because he had to talk about it one way or another, he would call Iris and persuade her over to his side. He had to persuade her, because she had implied a choice—take the money or the girl. Impossible. Because in a different way he loved them both.

He finished his second drink and then ordered a third on an empty stomach. The end of the third brought him to reckless rebellion, though underneath he was indecisive and lonely. All that money and he was lonely. So very goddam lonely.

And then a girl, dark-haired and middle tall, handsomely dressed in a turquoise sun dress, got up from the booth in front. He hadn't seen her come in. Which was strange, because he should have noticed her. In an unpremeditated sort of way she was a blantantly sensual type, a man's dream of a very long weekend.

She went by his booth, and their glances met. She had long lashes and wide slow eyes, exceedingly dark. They fell upon him with a cool envelopment. She was neither beautiful nor pretty, but somewhere between. There was angularity to her features, emphasized by the sweep of her hair into a psyche knot. The face was wide and high at the cheekbones, narrowing sharply to the small cleft of jaw so that it became a kind of cat face. She was also slim and long-legged and bosomy.

On the other hand, she was just another attractive girl in a town that chewed hundreds like her in the movie mill and spat them out upon the aprons of drive-in restaurants, where they became car hops. He dropped his eyes, and she went on.

He lifted his glass, drained it, munched pineapple. He looked up, and there she was again. Standing right beside his table now, looking down with an unsmiling expression of curious intentness. Her head was cocked. She might have been listening to the chiming of a distant clock for the hour. . . . There! The last note. And apparently the right one. For now she did smile. A thin, quiet smile.

Did he know her? He wasn't sure. There was a vague familiarity. She brought to mind some girl he might once have met briefly—a face lost in the complex of change.

"Please excuse me," she said. "I'm not in the habit of . . . But I certainly know you." She nodded. "Yes, I'm sure of it. I just can't grasp the name."

"Well," he said. "It would be a pleasure. But I'm afraid I can't place you."

"Sorry," she said. She began to move away, then came back snapping her fingers. "Got it! Don't you live at the Seaview Apartments on Ocean Avenue?"

"Why yes, I do."

"And so do I." Her smile brightened. "I was sure I had seen you."

"I must be dreaming lately," he said. "I never noticed you."

She nodded. "You did look preoccupied. You walked right past me—not a glance."

He laughed. "I'm Barry Lunsford. Sit down and have a drink."

She hesitated. "Well, I was just on my way back to the Seaview . . ."

"Did you drive?"

"No, I walked."

"Then I'll take you in my car."

She sat down. "They have very good chow mein here. About once a month I have a yen for it. Do you like chow mein?"

"Yes. But it never satisfies me. Half hour later, I'm hungry again." He signaled a waitress and ordered drinks, knowing one more would be too many for him, but feeling lonely and welcoming company.

She opened her purse and studied herself in the mirror on the back flap. Oblivious of him, she applied lipstick, then compressed her lips. She closed the purse. "My name is Vida," she said. "Vida Sattler. I live in Three-C. It's just a room and a bath with a kitchenette. That's all I need."

"I'm two floors up. In Five-A."

"Oh, lovely. Those are the big apartments with a view. Lovely. Expensive, though."

"Not very."

"Very," she said definitely. "If you're just an office girl like me. I never really saw one of those apartments, but I got a peek through an open door. I was impressed."

"I'd be glad to show you mine," he said. There was no motive in the offer, but her smile was sly.

"Would I be safe?"

"Pretty safe, I imagine."

The waitress brought the drinks, and for a moment they sipped in silence. Then he asked her questions about herself. She had always lived in California, she worked for a lumber company, was twenty-nine and divorced. He told her he was a partner in a small commercial film company. She said she had been told she was photogenic but had never tried for the movies. He was vague and evasive.

He still didn't feel like eating, so they had another drink and left. They got in his car and drove back to the apartment house in the early darkness. On the way she made much of the new convertible, exclaiming over its beauty and expense in an oddly bitter, my-my-don't-we-have-everything sort of manner. As though the one great importance was money and the things it could buy. As though she had always been cheated of her share.

Ordinarily her remarks would have irritated him. But he was high, on the verge of being tight. And he was only amused. If she understood the value of money, that was more than he could say for Iris. The hell with Iris. He was no longer lonely. He had found a kindred spirit.

In the elevator she said, "I won't stay but a minute. You must have things to do."

"Not tonight, Vida. You?"

"Well . . . I had a date. Last minute he had to fly to San Francisco on business."

"In that case, what's your hurry?"

She shrugged.

They stepped out of the elevator and walked down the hall. He opened his door and let her in. He turned on a lamp, and she made a little noise of delight, then moved around, touching furniture, pausing at the window facing the ocean.

"Charming," she said. "Look at the lights along the coast. From my place you can't see anything but the building next door. And the garbage cans."

He approached, studying the long inviting sweep of her back, then the profile lift of her breasts as she turned slightly toward him.

"You have an insatiable desire for nice things, don't you, Vida?" He was thinking clearly enough, but wondered whether his words weren't coming out a little fuzzy.

She gave him a sidelong glance. "Oh yes," she said, giggling. "It's—it's an obsession. My one weakness."

He felt reckless and powerful. She had so little and wanted so much. He needed to communicate with her, to be justified at last.

"If you had a lot of money," he said, "a whole lot, would you work?"

"Do I look crazy?" she snapped.

"And what about a man? If he has money, do you think he should feel compelled to work?"

She gave him a look of disdain. "Don't be silly. A man works to get money. After he gets all he needs, why should he work?"

"Only because people would say he's useless—a playboy." He lighted a cigarette and watched her.

She chuckled, a hard little sound. "People want you to work because *they* have to work. A guy who has money is a dope if he cares what anyone thinks."

He drew closer, and together they gazed into the night.

"Why do you talk so much about money?" she asked.

"Because I can tell it interests you."

"There's no use in talking about money, Barry, interested or not. With taxes the way they are, an honest person can't ever get rich. So then, how did you make your pile?"

"What pile?"

"You seem to have plenty." She turned to him, and her tone was mocking. "New car, beautiful apartment, fine clothes, a business of your own. Where did you steal it?"

"Does it matter?" He smiled.

"Uh-uh. Not to me."

"No Sunday school ethics?"

"Just one."

"What's that?"

"Don't get caught."

She grinned, but he knew she meant it. She bent

too far the other way, perhaps. She was probably amoral. But she was the refreshing change his mood demanded. They stood staring at each other, and he could almost hear the little ball of her thinking rotate precariously on the edge of decision, telling him to hurry and grab this isolated moment before it died and became something else.

He reached out and pulled her toward him. She came easily. Rag-doll limp. Head back, mouth open, eyes closed. He kissed her, and with a sound like a sob she tightened herself against him.

In a trance, they moved away from the window to the sofa and fell upon it. The kiss began again and went on and on. He fumbled with the snaps of her bra and got them open.

"Please," she said against his mouth. "Oh, please."

"You want me to stop?"

"Please hurry," she breathed.

He pulled the dress down, and her high distended breasts shimmered free. Then she stood and, watching his face with narrowed eyes, her long fingers unfastened, her body writhed—and she was naked.

"Why do you just sit there?" she said. "Don't you know there's a tide? Hurry, or you'll miss it. Hurry!"

He sat up in bed and looked at his watch when she came back from the bathroom, fully dressed. It was quarter of nine. "I'm hungry," he said.

"Naturally," she answered. "Men are always hungry—afterwards." Again she looked cool and contained.

"Sure, but I didn't have dinner."

"I could make you something. I'm hungry, too."

"Just a sandwich. There's ham and cheese and some roast beef."

"I'll find it," she said, moving languidly across the room to the door. "Take a nice long shower. I did. You'll feel better."

"Okay."

"How about coffee? You want coffee?"

"Sure."

She left, and he got out of bed. He put on a robe and went down the little hall to the bathroom. He closed the door, pulled the shower curtain across the tub and adjusted the taps. For a moment he sat on the clothes hamper, waiting for the hot water to come to temperature.

He wished now that Vida was gone and he could be with Iris. This was the great difference. Vida was sensational in bed, and that was all. Now he felt no rapport with her, had nothing to say to her. She was a stranger and would probably never be anything else, no matter how long he knew her. She was a body. Iris was a mentality, warm and communicating, known and lovable. She was also a body. But when the bodies tired of each other for a spell, the gap was filled. And this he understood to be love.

He stood, sighing, a little disgusted with himself, thinking that when Vida had gone he would call Iris and they would come to some compromise. He tested the water and was about to shed his robe and climb under when he decided to get his clothes and dress in the bathroom. Without the impulsion of sex, he had lost his taste for intimacy with Vida.

He left the water running and went out and down the hall.

She did not hear him approach. She was in the bedroom, going hastily through a bureau drawer. He stood in the doorway, watching. She closed the drawer and, finding his trousers on a chair, got his wallet and with quick nervous fingers examined his cash, ignored it, looked at papers, opened the change compartment.

His deposit box keys were in the compartment, and, while he did not want her to find them, he had to see if they produced a reaction.

She got them out and examined them closely. Then she clutched them in her fist, biting her lip, deep concentration and finally comprehension coming over her face.

He leaped into the room, caught her wrist and twisted until the keys fell into his palm. Her expression was a mixture of fear and defiance.

"Who are you?" he said. "What do you want with me? Answer!" He twisted the wrist again. "You hear me? Answer!"

"You're hurting me, you bastard," she hissed. "Let me go and I'll tell you."

He released her. She gave him a mighty slap, then a quick powerful shove off balance. She lunged away, down the hall to the door. Hurling it open, she went out a step ahead of him. He got halfway down the stairs before he realized that he was all but naked and couldn't follow.

He went back to the room and dressed frantically in slacks and sport shirt. Downstairs he beat rapidly on the door of apartment Three-C. But of course there was no answer.

"What girl in Three-C?" said Mr. Symons, the manager.

"A tall girl with dark hair. Twenty-nine, divorced, lives alone. Her name is Sattler. Vida Sattler."

Mr. Symons shook his head. "Some kind of mistake. No Vida Sattler here."

"Who's in Three-C?"

"Nobody, Mr. Lunsford. Nobody at all. Been empty nearly a month. Say—you all right? You don't look so good, Mr. Lunsford."

## CHAPTER NINE

HE FOUND HER purse on the night table, where she had left it in her haste. Surprisingly, there was absolutely nothing inside by way of identification. Lipstick, powder, mirror, comb. Seven dollars plus change. And a key.

The key was to a room in the Miramar Hotel, just a few blocks away.

He raced below and into his car. En route he unlocked the glove compartment and took from it a stubby .38 Smith and Wesson that he had bought and registered in Florida. Three minutes later he was in the lobby, taking the elevator to the fourth floor of the Miramar.

He searched down the corridor, and when he found the door he hesitated, listening.

He unlocked the door and went in.

The small room was orderly. And also vacant. Nothing in the closet, desk or bureau drawers. Two bobby pins and an empty bottle of nail polish on the night table. In the waste basket no scrap of paper—just a magazine. He reached for it.

It was one of the true crime publications, a current issue. He flipped the pages, caught sight of something and thumbed back to it. Three pages had been torn out roughly, pages 26 through 28. He made a mental note, tossed the magazine into the basket and left the room key on the bureau.

Returning to the lobby he bought a copy at the newsstand and turned to 26.

### MYSTERY CRIME OF THE YEAR

*How did the Jacksonville armored car bandits steal a million, murder three guards and go scot-free?*

Perhaps the most brutal and sensational crime of its kind in history, the Jacksonville armored car robbery, still rests in the files of local and Federal officials, stamped *Unsolved*. Even among the diehards of the FBI, there is a growing belief that so clever was the planning behind this spectacular assault of an armored car that the criminals and their "M.O." may never become known.

One of the most puzzling aspects of the crime is the manner in which . . .

Lunsford tucked the magazine in his pocket and hurried to the desk.

"You have a Miss Vida Sattler registered?" he asked the clerk.

"No, sir. She just checked out."

"How long?"

"Couldn't be much more than five minutes."

"She leave a forwarding?"

"No, sir. But—are you Mr. Barnum?"

"That's right," he said quickly. "I'm Barnum."

"Well, just a minute. She left a message for you."

The clerk turned and, producing an envelope, handed it over.

"Thanks," Lunsford said. He walked off, slitting the envelope, upon which there was nothing but the name C. Barnum blocked in pencil.

The message was on hotel stationery. A single line, frantically printed.

TROUBLE WITH L. MEET YOU LATER AT THE SHORE.
V.

He stuck the note in his pocket. With endless miles of shore, it was meaningless. In a couple of minutes, with the help of the bell captain, he had located the boy who had carried the bag down from Room 412.

"I'm trying to find the lady who checked out of Four-twelve," said Lunsford. "I just missed her. Can you tell me where she was going?"

"No, sir. She didn't say."

"Did she leave by taxi?"

"No, sir. I carried the bag to her car. The lady,

she was in a big hurry. Run my legs off. For nothin'. Know what I mean? I'm skinny enough that I don't need no free exercise. That's what I tole 'er."

Lunsford gave the bellhop a buck, and he grinned suddenly.

"You say she had her own car? What sort of car?"

"New Ford. Black sedan."

"Anything else you remember about it?"

"No, sir. A Ford is a Ford. Had Florida plates."

"Florida? You sure?"

"Positive. You don't see many of them traitors here."

"Which way did she go?"

"Can't say. I was pooped out and didn't give it no mind."

"Much obliged," said Lunsford.

He drove home mechanically, thinking about the missing pages from the fact-crime magazine and the black Ford with the Florida plates.

He was unlocking the door to his apartment when Vida came back to him in full frame. She did not really look like anyone he had ever met in the hazy complex of the past. She looked more like a girl seen briefly from the side of a road in Florida.

A girl driving a black Ford sedan; approaching slowly from behind as he inspected the tire of the Chevy; gazing curiously at him before she disappeared across the railroad track.

## CHAPTER TEN

HE MADE himself a stiff drink, brought it to the phone in the bedroom and dialed Iris.

"Good to hear your voice, Barry," she said. "I was wondering if—"

"Why didn't you call me?"

"Well, there was nothing to say, really. I wanted you to have enough time to realize that—"

"Sure. Sure, I know." He gulped from the glass. "To tell you the truth, Iris, I still thought you were wrong. Dead wrong. Up until an hour ago. Then I changed my mind."

"Did something happen?"

"Oh, you're so damn right!"

He told her about Vida, explaining that she had deceived him by pretending she wanted to see his apartment. He sidestepped the sex angle neatly in the telling.

"Oh God, it's frightening," said Iris. "Then the money came from that armored car robbery."

"It would be a good bet. Of course, just because

that article was missing from the magazine ... That doesn't die it down for keeps, you know. But when you place this Vida in Florida and at that railroad crossing, well ..."

"But how did the money get there below the track, Barry?"

"Looks to me like Vida Sattler, which is probably not her real name, was toting the money in the car. Then maybe she saw the cops just ahead with that license check roadblock. Probably she got panicky and tossed the case out the window. Chances are that when I saw her she was coming back to pick it up. She could have gone through the line and doubled back."

"Of course!" said Iris. "And when she saw you she may have become suspicious, and then she—"

"Made a note of my license number?"

"Exactly."

"Well, that gets her to my old address. But how she traced me out to L.A. beats me. She must have had plenty of help."

"That's the part that scares me, Barry. The help she had. Those men killed three guards in that truck. At least I assume there was more than one man involved."

"Had to be."

"Do you suppose they've been trailing you around and checking you for some time?"

"My God, I don't know. I imagine so. They had to be sure, so they used Vida as a spy. Young girl, apparently innocent and harmless. Ha!"

"Darling, what are you going to do?"

"Just what you wanted me to in the first place."

"Take it to the police?"

"God almighty," he sighed. "All that money. I'd like to grab it and head for Mexico. The rest of my life I'll be just another slob chasing a buck in the goddam stinking treadmill. Hundred or so a week—here, Uncle, take your big cut and drop it like confetti all over Europe and Asia and South America. I dunno, baby, I just can't see it."

"Barry dear—don't. Please don't get yourself all worked up in the wrong direction again. When will you go to the police?"

"I'll sleep on it, honey. Then in the morning, maybe..."

"Go now! Barry. Go right now."

"Iris! God damn it, please don't make up my mind for me. You think I can reverse myself just like that—take three hundred thousand bucks and flush it down the drain? Kiss it good-by and say it would have been fun, boys, but that's the way the dollar crumbles? Remembering of course, my Boy Scout oath to help old ladies across the street and turn all found money over to the cops so they can shoot crap for it in some musty back room of a police station. Right?"

He bolted down a giant slug. His hand was shaking.

"Barry, listen to me. On account of that money, three men died."

"Possibly."

"And you could be the fourth."

"Possibly."

"So will you please do it?" Her voice came soft and pleading, on the brink of tears. "Because I love you and I don't want anything to happen to you. Please?"

He was silent, rotating the glass violently, listening to the rattle of ice.

"Are you there, Barry?"

"All right, honey. In the morning. Oh God, God."

"You won't go *now?*"

"Can't. I'm washed out. Couldn't cope with it all. I need sleep."

"But in the morning?"

"The morning. And, Iris?"

"Yes, darling."

"I'm sorry. About the scrap we had. I love you, kiddo."

"Oh, Barry, Barry. I knew you did. And I see your side. I understand that it's an awfully hard decision."

"A tough one, sweetie. A beaut. Call you in the morning."

"In the morning, Barry."

" 'By, kiddo."

He dropped the receiver in place and slugged the rest of the highball down. Then, for a long time, he sat thinking. After a while he felt better.

He went out to the kitchen to get something to eat.

## CHAPTER ELEVEN

HE HAD STRIPPED down to his shorts and was in the bathroom brushing his teeth when the phone rang. He dropped the brush into the little slot, spat and sloshed a handful of water across his mouth. He grabbed a towel and, wiping his face and hands, strode into the bedroom to answer. He caught it in the middle of the fourth ring.

"Yes?"

"Lunsford?"

"Yeah, who's this?"

"A friend of Vida's. Know what I mean?" A male voice, low-pitched, cool.

"No. I don't know what you mean."

"Don't, eh? Well, let me explain it. I'll spell it out for ya in big red letters. We want the dough. Got the message?"

"What dough?"

"Tomorrow when the bank opens, you take those keys and you go down and open that box. Then you take that three hundred grand and you bring it back there and you wait. You'll hear from us. Got it?"

"Sure. Any time some guy calls me on the phone and asks for money, I always see that he gets all he wants."

"You have a brave sound there, pal. Are you a hero?"

"Listen, who the hell are you?"

"Tomorrow. When the bank opens. Don't forget. Or you'll be a sorry boy."

"What's in it for me?"

"A hole in the head, thirty-eight caliber."

The line went dead.

He stood there with the phone in his hand, trembling. He wasn't brave at all—at least, no more than average. If he was brave, why was he afraid? Of course, the head shrinkers said that fear was no sign of cowardice. Courage was a matter of doing what had to be done in spite of fear. In such a jam, only an idiot would be fearless. A man never knew what he was made of until he was tested. In the Army he had been Signal Corps, headquarters, far behind the lines. His life had never been on the block. He hadn't been tried.

He wasn't ready now.

He put the phone down and went into the living room. He checked the door. Locked. The chain was in place. He was five floors of sheer wall from the ground. The windows didn't matter, but he locked them anyway.

He got the gun out of a drawer, inspected it and placed it under his pillow. For several minutes he sat on the bed, staring at the phone. There would be the late-night, slightly bored, doubtful voice of the cop who answered. His fantastic story, told on the phone, would have the sound of a nut, a borderline psycho. They might send someone to investigate—probably radio a squad car. And, if the clever shadows were lurking in the darkness, they would vanish and the cops would find nothing. They would ask questions and they would take notes, concealing their disbelief, telling him to bring his story and the money to the detective bureau in the morning. Then they would go away and he would be just as vulnerable. Anyhow, he was safe enough until he failed to obey.

Wearing only his shorts, he got into bed and put out the light. He listened. But, with the windows closed, he was wrapped in silence. Once he got up and for a long time sat in the darkness, watching the street. There was nothing. He went back to bed.

He thought of calling Iris. There would be a certain comfort in sharing trouble. But a selfish comfort. She would be scared—for him. Wide-eyed through the night.

He thought of going himself to the police station, remaining until morning. But getting there was the risk. The danger.

He knew he wasn't going to sleep. He was prepared for it, conditioned to lie rigid on his back. Sleepless. For that very reason he was later puzzled to feel the bright intense glare of sunlight on his closed lids and to realize that he had slept after all.

and into morning. Perhaps too long. And too late.

So that his eyes flew open and he might have jumped up suddenly. Except that, for the space of a heartbeat after first vision, he delayed. The sun seemed so harshly white and coldly blinding. Incongruous because it came like a narrow cone flung from darkness.

In any case, he could not have moved without losing an eye. Because the knife point gleamed dead center of his pupil, held by a gloved hand that was bodiless behind the big flashlight. And the barrel of the gun in another gloved hand was at his temple.

The voice, coming at him distantly, was also disembodied. "A guy could wake up in the morgue and get the same charge—eh, Lunsford?" It was a hoarse whisper.

He didn't answer; he couldn't.

"Now be a hero," hissed the other with the gun. "Tell us you'll hold out, you bastard. Tell us you won't go like a nice boy to that bank and bring back the cash. C'mon, be brave for us."

"All right, all right," he choked. "You'll get the money."

"He's lying," said the other with the gun. "Impress him."

The sheet was ripped off him, and the point of the knife touched his bare chest under the collarbone. "Not a sound or you're gone." He knew it was coming and clamped his lip. The pressure increased and the knife was drawn slowly down the center of his body. So sharp was the blade that he felt only a burning, a long slice of flame. Yet, when he looked, small lips of flesh had been opened all the way to the groin. Bright blood welled from the valley of the incision, a narrow river of crimson overflowing from torn banks of tissue.

He caught the sob in his throat and held it there. The hand wiped the bloody knife across his face.

"It's like a side of beef you know, Lunsford. You make a cut. It's the line you wanna follow. And the next time, the last time, you understand, you slice right on through. And what've you got then? You got half a man, right, Lunsford? You remember that next time. And you get that dough. And when you get it and before you get it and after you get it, you're a goddam dummy. A mute. No tongue. None at all. Right? Answer!"

"Oh Christ. Yes, I'll be a goddam dummy and I'll—"

The phone rang. The room became a frozen cube in which there was only that isolated sound.

"Pick it up, Lunsford. Talk sleepy and sign off fast. Make it good. Answer!"

"It's—it's Iris, Barry."

"Half asleep. Call back in the morning, huh?"

"Barry, I—I got worried." She sounded odd, guilty. "And I—I called the police."

"That's good. Good idea." Was there ever a better one! The knife point touched his throat. "But it's the middle of the night. Talk tomorrow." He held the receiver tight against his ear.

He looked down. Blood was running off at the

sides of the wound, across his chest and belly onto the sheets. He felt a gray dizziness, a sweaty nausea.

"Barry, the police were here. Two detectives from Homicide. Sergeant Kieffer and Detective Gurney. They just left and—and they'll be over. I was so scared, and I thought that—"

"Okay, Iris. Fine." The point of the knife told him to shut up. "Be in touch tomorrow."

He hung up. God, it was an unbelievable break. The police coming over. How strange he must have sounded. Nothing mattered, though. He was too shaken, too sick.

"Who was that? Who's Iris?"

He looked into the light, turned his head away. "Just a girl friend."

"What's she want, this hour?"

"She was at a party. She was looped. Just talk."

The light moved, and he heard the phone cord being jerked from its mooring.

"There! That'll take care of the phone. And listen, you creep. Make a move in any direction and we'll be watching. Don't try it. Get the money. Or else!"

Then they were gone, backing from the room, the flash tight on his face. He heard the door close softly. And he was alone in darkness.

He began to shiver, feeling the blood wetness of his body. And the horror that was in him came out in a dry retching and sobbing.

## CHAPTER TWELVE

IN A MINUTE he put on the light. Dripping blood, he went into the bathroom and washed the long incision. With the blood gone, it was not as bad as it had appeared during the eerie terror of that bedroom nightmare. It was a shallow surface cut, and already the bleeding had diminished. Wincing, gritting his teeth, he applied iodine. He scissored a narrow strip from an old sheet and, with tape and gauze from his medicine kit, fixed a makeshift bandage. He washed the long smear of the knife from his cheek and went back to the bedroom.

He changed his bloodstained shorts and dressed quickly. He looked around for the phone, thinking he might reconnect the cord to the terminals. He couldn't find the instrument. They must have taken it with them.

He looked at his watch. Twenty minutes before 1 A.M. He went into the living room and put on some lights. Then he inspected the door. Astonishingly, there was no sign of tampering with the lock.

Similarly, the chain dangled, undisturbed. They were experts. They must have known some tricks with which he was unfamiliar.

He reset the lock and chain. In the kitchen he poured bourbon on the rocks, then went back to the living room and sat down, facing the door, to wait. He drank deeply and felt relief, though the shudder was still in him and his calm wouldn't return.

Thank God for Iris. She was presumptuous and headstrong to have called the police. She might have trusted him. But, anyway, thank God for Iris. Being men, it was inevitable that the police would give more attention to an attractive girl.

Now that those thugs were gone, he wondered what he might have done. Would he have brought them the money without tipping the police? In the fear of that moment, he would have promised anything. But later, in daylight, he would have changed his mind. He was certain of it. He'd have gone into the bank, and the minute he was out of sight he'd have called the police. They would have come and taken him to the station with the money, and it would have been over. Nothing left for those bastards but vengeance. Would they risk a profitless killing? Likely not, if they had been clever enough to steal a fortune from an armored car. And of course the police would have sent men to guard him for a time. Especially since, if these were the armored car criminals, this was a very big deal in the annals of crime.

If these hoods were so brilliant, why couldn't

they figure out the possibility that he might stall and then give them away from the bank? It didn't make sense. Could they have a plan to cover that eventuality, too?

Sure. Look how cleverly they were working. A girl to check him out, leaving their identities unknown to him. A sprawling city like L.A. and they had found him. They open a door without making a sound or leaving a mark. They stand behind a powerful flashlight and remain invisible throughout a controlled terrorizing that left him mentally shocked but still capable of physical obedience. Brutal but purposeful, whatever joys of brutality there were merely incidental to the plan.

So then, would they leave anything to guesswork? Would they gamble that he would not inform the cops once in the bank? Never. Not these types. What then? How were they going to protect every avenue?

It didn't matter now. The element of the unforeseen, the impossible to calculate—like Iris compelled by her emotional torment to summon help—worked always in favor of the law. And, if she had called just a half hour earlier, it would all be over now—or two cops would be very dead.

He had poured a second drink, flamed a fresh cigarette and was feeling no less unnerved when the bell rang.

The sound jarred him. He knew the others would not ring the bell. And yet he felt a reluctance to answer. He set down glass and cigarette and got up slowly, moving to the door, cautiously parting the spy flap.

Two men in gray and brown business suits. Early thirties. Casual undisturbed faces, full of cynical patience.

"Yes?"

"Mr. Lunsford?"

"Yes."

"Police officers. Miss Howland called us. Iris Howland."

He opened the door.

"May we come in, sir?"

He nodded and they entered, waiting a little awkwardly in the center of the room. Standing silent and solemn, watching him with a kind of indirection.

They were big men, and youthful. Neither had the paunchy, flabby look that made the bellied sort of policeman look incongruous in a job connected with force and violence.

No, both these men had the look of capability and lithe hardness, and Lunsford felt as though he had come out of a jungle into security.

"I'm Sergeant Kieffer, Homicide. And this is Detective Gurney."

Neither offered a hand, but Lunsford extended his, and they each took it with a half smile. Kieffer, a dark blond man who was taller than his companion by not more than an inch, had a face heavy but solid, round and flat at the cheeks, long at the jaw. The contour was odd, yet gave him a look of special forcefulness. He had no-fooling-around eyes, dark and unblinking. But perhaps this was his official manner. He seemed conscious of authority.

Gurney had black hair and a narrower build, a supple grace. He was good-looking in spite of a slightly hooked nose and a mouth too wide and full. He seemed the more easygoing of the two; he had about him an air of good nature spiced with arrogance. He had long-lashed, pale-blue eyes that he sometimes squinted, as though reading small print at too great a distance, and the kind of beard shadow that shaving would never quite erase.

Kieffer opened his coat, and, when he searched his trousers for a cigarette, his holstered service weapon became visible. He gave himself a light, puffed and compressed his lips.

"Had to stop by the station on the way," he said. "Held us up a little. Gave you a call, but the line was out of order."

"I know," said Lunsford. "I'll explain why in a minute. Won't you sit down?"

They sat. Gurney yawned.

"Drink?"

"Sure," said Gurney, smiling. Kieffer gave him a look.

"No drinks," said the Sergeant.

Lunsford sat, and Kieffer crossed his legs, pulling at his trousers. "The little girl, uh . . . Miss Howland, she seems to think you got troubles. Now is this lady friend of yours just a little hysterical? I mean, is she an excitable type or is there really something to this business? You got three hundred thousand in a safety deposit box, the Bank of America. You found this money in Florida. My God. You just found it. And then you come out here and you meet some cookie in a bar and she comes up to your apartment and you catch her snooping around. And she beats it and you go to her hotel room and you find her checked out, but she's left a magazine behind with pages torn out concerning a robbery-homicide, an armored car in Jacksonville. And you think maybe this baby and her mob have come out here looking for you and the loot. My Christ, how much of this is true, Mr. Lunsford?"

"All of it. Every bit."

The two men looked at each other.

"You have this money, this three hundred grand you say you found, in the bank?" Kieffer leaned forward, frowning.

"That's right."

"Well, now." For the first time, Kieffer really grinned. "It's hard not to believe a man who has all that dough to back up his story. You might be onto something at that. New bills or old?"

"Old."

"All of them?" asked Gurney.

"Yes, all of them. Some twenties. But mostly fifties and hundreds."

"Old money," mused Kieffer. "That's bad. If it was new, we could trace it. Now, when you found this money, what did you do about it? Did you make some attempt to locate the owner?"

"Well, I called the police department in Miami

and asked if they had any report on it. They said no. And I watched the papers for an ad. Nothing."

"But," said Kieffer, "you didn't actually take the money into the police department and explain the whole story, did you?"

"No."

"Three hundred thousand smackers," said Gurney, shaking his head and giving a low whistle.

"That's what you should of done," said Kieffer sternly. "You should of turned the money over to the police. They would of given you a receipt for it. You'd get it back after a time if the crooks who stole it didn't turn up in the investigation. Now why didn't you do that, sir?"

"Would you? I mean as an ordinary citizen, not a policeman?"

Again Gurney and Kieffer looked at each other. Kieffer couldn't hold back the smile, and Gurney laughed frankly. "Well, I won't answer that," said Kieffer. "On the grounds it might incriminate me. All right. So technically you should of done one thing but you did another. All right. We'll start from there. Now suppose you tell us the whole story in your own words. I don't want nothing secondhand."

He told them briefly. Gurney nodded, and Kieffer established a pyramid with his fingers and pursed his lips. "But," Lunsford said, hurrying on, "the really important part happened just before you came. I had gone to bed and I fell asleep. I woke up suddenly, and there was this powerful light in my face and I ..."

He gave a detailed accounting.

"My Christ," said Kieffer.

"The bastards," said Gurney.

"Open your shirt please, sir," said Kieffer. "And lemme have a look."

He unbuttoned the shirt. Both men came to his chair, and he pulled a section of bandage away carefully.

"Well, it's not very deep," said Kieffer. "Still bleeding a little. I see you put iodine on. Good. But maybe tomorrow you ought to have some doc take a squint, huh?"

"Crazy sadists," said Gurney. "Psychos."

"No," said Kieffer. "Not necessarily. These guys are sharp operators. They wanted to toss a good scare, show they meant business—and they did."

"They might be out there now," said Lunsford. "Waiting and watching."

"Could be," said Gurney.

"Didn't see anyone when we came in," Kieffer said. "But we'll scout around good on the way out. Well . . . this puts the lid on. Could very well be that armored car bunch. I'm gonna stake this place out the rest of the night and see if those mugs come back. We'll do it in a way they won't know we're on tap."

"I don't mind telling you," said Lunsford, "I'm not in love with the idea of staying here, sweating it out till dawn alone."

"Maybe we should take him in for safekeeping," said Gurney.

"No," Kieffer answered. "I'll have a couple of men out of sight on the landing above. No one will get by them. All right. Now, Mr. Lunsford, in the morning you go down to the bank and get the money. You've got to turn it in, anyway. The stuff is blood-filthy, you can be sure. And, old or not, our lab might just come up with something on it. We'll have that whole area of Santa Monica near the bank surrounded, and, if they try to pull something cute, we've got 'em. We'll be watching, but if you happen to see us, you don't give us so much as a wink—just keep moving.

"Now here's the way we'll work it. When you go down to the bank, you park your car in the lot behind it on that side street. You know the one?"

"Sure. About half a block west of the bank. I always park there."

"Good. What kind of a car you got?"

"New Pontiac convertible. White with a white top."

Kieffer nodded, "So, after you get the money, you get in your car with it, and you drive out of the lot and head for here. We'll be somewhere behind all the way in a plain black police Chevy, no insignia. Other cars will be along the route, and we'll be in touch by radio. The idea, of course, is to see if you're being tailed. If so, before you get home, we'll have 'em boxed off and we'll take 'em in custody. Got it?"

"Suppose they try to grab the money?" asked Lunsford.

"Chances are they won't. But, if so, don't risk your neck. Hand it over and then let us collar the bastards before they get a block. Ya see?"

"I see, sure. And it's all very neat. But I don't like being a decoy—especially a dead one."

"Ahhh," said the sergeant. "Don't panic. You'll never be out of sight. Just keep cool all the way. But then, when you get here, don't stop. Because by this time we'll know you're not being followed. You go on past, and you turn the next corner and go east two blocks. You pull up to the curb and you stop. We catch up and you get in with us, and we take the money down to the station. I get a change of plans from upstairs, I'll send word to you. Otherwise, it stands. Okay?"

Lunsford stared.

"He don't wanna give up that cash," said Gurney.

"Christ, I don't blame him," said Kieffer sympathetically. "And I wish I could promise you'll get it back. You might. And then again I doubt it. Because that much money don't lie around unless it's got tilt stamped all over it."

"I'll worry about the money when those guys are in jail," said Lunsford.

"Tomorrow then," said Kieffer. "Time it so you reach the bank at ten on the button. And don't you worry—this place will be staked out tonight and you'll be safe enough."

"All right," said Lunsford. "I don't like it, but all right. I don't like anything about this mess." He got up too fast, forgetting the cut, and felt the sharp pain of it down his chest.

He let the officers out, shaking hands with them in the doorway.

"Get some sleep," said Kieffer. "My Christ, but you've had a night, eh boy?"

"Luck," said Gurney.

He watched them go down the hall to the elevator, then went back inside. It was almost laughable, but he locked and chained himself in. Then he got the gun from under the pillow, went back and sank into a chair facing the door. He left the lights on.

This time he wasn't going to fall asleep.

## CHAPTER THIRTEEN

AT 9:30 that morning, Lunsford got the big salesman's brief case and began to stuff it with the bare essentials for a short stay at some motel. Once the police had the money, his part was over. He wasn't going to spend another night in that apartment until he had reason to feel safe. He was already anticipating the next demand upon him. They would want him to remain in the apartment until he got a message telling him where to deliver the money. The police would tail him at a careful distance—too careful and too distant—and he would be a lure for the killers. No thanks. The hell with that. His co-operation went just so far. However, he couldn't carry a suitcase, because that would give away his intent if anyone were watching.

On top of the clothing and toilet articles, he placed a laundry bag. He would carry his belongings to the room in this. At a motel, who cared? Then, as he was closing the case, the idea came to him quite naturally. Why not transfer the money to the laundry bag, leave it in the trunk and carry the case full of his clothing on the seat? Then, if someone tried to hold him up for the cash, all they'd get would be a few bucks' worth of clothes.

Ready now, he picked up the .38 and studied it thoughtfully. He had no intention of using it in a stupid gun battle for money that wasn't going to be his any longer. But he would lock it in the glove compartment; it would be a small comfort once he was again on his own. He dropped it into his coat pocket.

At quarter to ten, carrying the brief case, he went out.

There were a couple of men across the avenue in the little park. They strolled along slowly and did not look his way. He could not tell if they were friend or enemy. Another man was sitting on a bench, watching nothing but his shoes.

He climbed in the Pontiac, put the gun in the glove compartment and locked it from temptation. They wanted the money, not his life. They could have the money. He placed the briefcase next to him on the seat and drove off.

If he was followed on his way to the bank, he was not able to detect it. Sooner or later the most persistent of cars on his tail wheeled in other directions.

He parked in the lot west of the bank, opened the case and placed the laundry bag on the floor. On top of it he dumped the clothing. He rolled up the windows and pushed the door buttons. He got out and made sure the car was locked. He took the ticket from the lot attendant and walked briskly toward the bank.

It was a fine day, crisp and clear with a brisk wind from the ocean blowing the interminable smog from the sky. A winter sun dispensed heat with moderation and spread a brightness upon the streets and buildings that rebuked the possibility of crime and danger.

Nevertheless, as Barry Lunsford entered the bank, he was nervous. Crossing to the desk before the deposit vault, he felt as though he had walked on-stage and all eyes were following his progress under a brilliant spot. Yet no one seemed to be paying him the least attention.

The girl gave him a card. He signed, and she checked his signature in the file. She opened the door and he followed her to his box. She turned her master key in one lock and gave his own a twist in the other. She withdrew the box and handed it to him. He took it to a cubicle and, behind the door, filled the case. A minute later he was again on the street.

He carried the case snug under his arm. Three hundred thousand, and he no longer gave a damn what happened to it as long as he wasn't caught in the middle. He almost wished he could give it to the crooks who stole it so that he could get them off his back forever. And yet, remembering the three guards who might have died for this and the remaining six hundred forty thousand, he knew that he wanted them caught and dispatched in the electric chair at Raiford Prison in Florida.

Three hundred twenty thousand was . . . exactly one-third of nine hundred sixty grand! Why hadn't he thought of that before? If there had been a three-way split . . .

The thought evaporated with the sight of Sergeant Kieffer and his partner, Gurney. They were just across the street, coming from a restaurant. They must have been sitting in a booth behind the glass, facing the street, watching. He felt reassured at sight of them.

He turned the corner toward the lot, and a police car cruised slowly past. Two men came out of the lot and moved in his direction. The chunky one was chewing a toothpick and talking from the side of his mouth. Lunsford felt himself tightening. He walked swiftly, and when he was on top of them they didn't give ground and he thought, This is it! But he sidestepped around them, and they shoved on.

He looked over his shoulder. The chunky one had done an about-face and was yanking the other's arm. Now they both moved purposefully after him. He tried to keep his head, wishing he had the gun. Nowhere was there a sign of Kieffer or Gurney.

He began to hurry, almost running. He swung into the lot, gave the attendant half a buck, told him to keep it and raced to his car. He was unlocking the door and tossing the case inside when he saw the two men approaching. They never reached him. Three cars away, they paused while the chunky one opened the door to a Buick and removed a large package wrapped in brown paper. Carrying this, he moved off with his companion, and they left the lot.

Lunsford decided that the man had simply left a package and they had returned for it. Every person, and the most innocent action, seemed hostile when you were carrying three hundred thousand dollars.

He locked himself in, quickly dumped the money from the case into the laundry bag, filled the case with his clothing and turned the little key in the lock. Checking to see that he was unobserved, he opened the trunk, tossed the bag in and slammed the lid.

As he gunned from the lot and swung west, he watched his mirror. A black Chevy pulled from the curb and followed, well back. That should be Kieffer and Gurney, though at that distance he couldn't tell.

He kept the windows closed and the doors locked. He drove without haste, and the black car was never long out of sight. It was all neatly done, because, although he saw two squad cars, he never did see another of those black Chevies like the one behind him. He supposed other detectives in unmarked cars were moving along different routes, ready to be summoned by radio.

He crossed to Wilshire and remained there in the comparative safety of heavy traffic. Two minutes, and he had turned on Ocean Avenue. He slid past the Seaview and saw no one except the idlers on the Promenade. He made the turn at the next corner, rolled east for two blocks and braked at the curb. The tension left him. There had really been nothing to it after all. He cranked the windows open and took a deep breath.

In the mirror he watched the approach of the black car, thinking miserably that in a few minutes he would lose irrevocably over three hundred thousand dollars, wondering whether they would find a way to make him pay back even the few thousand he had spent. He would soon be broke again, and the whole crazy business would have been for nothing.

The black Chevy drew closer, and still he couldn't make out the men on the front seat. For a wild moment he thought perhaps it might not be Kieffer and Gurney after all. He got the motor started again and set the shift arm for drive. But then the car came abreast, and Kieffer, on the passenger side, gave him a tight nod and a wink. Lunsford cut the motor.

Kieffer got out, opened the back door of the Chevy and stood there, waiting. Lunsford handed him the briefcase with a grin. Might as well make a little joke about the money, kid them along. Kieffer looked at the case with something like reverence and placed it on the front seat. Lunsford went around back to open the trunk. The Chevy was pulled slightly ahead, and, as he glanced at the rear, taking in the California plate, his eye caught something shiny, above on the deck, that caused him to freeze in place.

On the lower edge of the trunk lid, in chrome letters:

        WILTON CHEVROLET
        JACKSONVILLE, FLA.

## CHAPTER FOURTEEN

"C'MON!" SAID Kieffer. "What the hell you doin?"

"Damn trunk comes open sometimes," Lunsford said, stalling. "Bad lock. Just checking."

His mind whirled. He didn't know what to do. It was insane. Iris had sent these cops herself. But it was all wrong. He'd have to play it by ear.

He gave the trunk lid a final pull and walked to the Chevy. In the front seat, Gurney's hand was resting on the case, his thumb pushing vainly on the lock catch. In his other hand he was clutching a .38. It wasn't exactly aimed at Lunsford, but it hovered in his direction. Kieffer had his coat open, and his hand was resting on the butt of the weapon in his holster.

"Listen," said Lunsford to Kieffer, "why don't you go ahead with the money and I'll follow. That way I'll have my car at the station and I can drive myself back. Case anyone's around, it'll look better if I'm alone."

"No," said Kieffer. "You come with us. You'll be a lot safer."

They had what they thought was the money and still that wasn't enough. They wanted him. He knew too much. And could identify them.

"I'll be okay," he answered, forcing a grin. "I made it this far, didn't I?"

"Don't argue," snapped Kieffer. "For the time being, consider yourself under arrest." Gurney had brought the gun up higher, so that the barrel stared at him from the seat, without appearing to threaten.

"Arrest?" said Lunsford. "I don't understand."

"Nothing to it," said Kieffer more pleasantly. "We'll just have you in safekeeping. Like a material witness."

"Oh," said Lunsford, pretending complete comprehension. "I thought you meant something different. Well, if I'm going to be gone awhile and I can't take the car, I'll just lock 'er up tight." He moved toward the Pontiac as though to question such a natural act would be absurd.

"Snap it up!" said Kieffer.

Lunsford waved and climbed into the Pontiac, giving the door a little help so that it swung shut behind him. He closed the near window and shoved the door button down. Both quarter windows were up. He leaned far across the wide seat, bending down a fraction more than required to crank the passenger window.

The keys were in his hand. He thought of the gun locked in the glove compartment. And knew instantly it would be a suicide try. Besides, there was still a small doubt in his mind. Could they be genuine cops sent from Jacksonville?

He shoved the key in the lock and depressed the accelerator. Start! he prayed. For God's sake, start! Still bent across the seat, he gave the key a twist. The starter whined, and the motor caught. He pulled the gear arm into drive just as the first shot came blasting through the window and into the floorboard. Kieffer loomed at the window, taking more careful aim. Lunsford sank lower, held the wheel and jammed the accelerator.

The Pontiac leaped ahead, and the second shot struck the dash. He raised his head just in time to swerve around a parked car. There was another shot, but he didn't hear it strike. He was already climbing past sixty, wondering whether some insight had caused him to buy, not the most expensive car, but the fastest. Pontiac had won that year's stock car race. Accelerating, gave him the feeling that, with a yard of wing span, he could catapult himself into the air.

Behind him, Kieffer had climbed into the Chevy, and Gurney was hurling the car in pursuit. Ahead he saw the green Plymouth approaching from the side street. He was doing seventy, and there was no stopping now. He palmed the horn ring and held it down. The woman was dead center of the road, eyes wide, mouth gaping toward him. At the last second, she made the Plymouth frog-jump ahead, and he slid past her rear bumper with inches to spare.

A block beyond, the light at the intersection flicked from yellow to red. He braked to a sliding, swaying stop. Heavy traffic, as though loosed like bees from a bottle neck, swarmed south and buzzed north. It was a hopeless jam, with no time for turning around. The black Chevy was plunging into range, and Kieffer was sighting out his window.

To get the glove compartment open Lunsford would have to cut the motor, because the key was on the same ring with the one in the ignition switch. Frantically, he tried to decide. Gun battle, two against one, or—what?

Then he saw the hole opening. Between the oncoming truck from the north and the Lincoln sedan, south. Ten yards and closing, but . . . He gassed the Pontiac to the floor. It reared back and flew into the crossing. Horns blared, brakes squealed. He skinned past the Lincoln, swerved left around the truck and back into lane. The pulse of traffic behind paused for a beat, then roared on angrily in a solid wall of vehicles. The Chevy was caught.

He plowed ahead, wheeled right, then left, zigzagging over to Wilshire. This time the light was green, and he surged across. Half a block on the other side, he came to the service entrance of an Olds dealer. He swung in sharply and, when the man came with his clipboard of order sheets, told him to have the oil changed. And he could use a grease job, too.

Meanwhile, he sat on a leather couch in back of the showroom and tried vainly to reduce the thumping pace of his heart.

## CHAPTER FIFTEEN

AN HOUR later he had redeposited the money in a safety box at still another bank—this one in Westwood. He had then traveled east on Olympic until he found a motel and checked in. From the public booth outside he called Iris at the office, but she wasn't there. He found her at home.

"Barry—where are you?"

"My God, I wouldn't even tell *you* after what's happened to me since last night. Who the hell were those phony cops you sent over?"

"Phony?"

"Damn right! Just tell me this. When you called in, what station did you call?"

"Why I—I called Santa Monica, because—"

"You're sure?"

"Yes, I—I'm positive."

"You don't sound it."

"I'm nervous. I kept phoning and couldn't get you."

"But it was the Santa Monica police you called?"

"Yes."

"Kieffer and Gurney?"

"That's right, Barry."

"Both tall, in their thirties, black-haired guy and a dark blond?"

"Yes, uh . . . Detective Gurney is the black-haired one and Sergeant Kieffer—"

"Well, I'll be damned! Did they mention being sent from Florida, anything like that?"

"No. No, they didn't. How did you know I was home from work?"

"I called the office, naturally. They said you were sick."

"Don't be angry, Barry. I'm—I'm only trying to help." She choked back a sob, and he melted.

"Of course you're trying to help, honey. Now don't cry. Something is wrong here that I can't understand. Terribly wrong."

"Won't you explain?" She sounded still on the verge of tears.

"Not now. I've got to make another call right away."

"Barry, dear. After that will you come over? This whole business has me frightened sick. I mean it. Will you please come over so we can talk?"

"Maybe. Depends on what I find out."

"Please?"

"Maybe. To tell the truth I'm beginning to wonder about everyone. Even about . . ."

"Me?"

"Yes."

"Barry!"

"All right, we'll see. Probably within the hour. Just probably."

"Why don't you bring the money, Barry. We'll go to the police station together with it—get this whole thing straightened out."

"No. The money's safe. No more games."

"Barry, you couldn't possibly think that I—"

"Later, Iris. Later. I'm in a hurry."

"Well, where did you put—"

He hung up.

Now he searched the directory for the Santa Monica police and dialed. He got the police operator and was switched to the Detective Bureau.

"I'd like to speak to Detective Sergeant Kieffer, Homicide."

"He's not in, sir."

He was, for a moment, without speech.

"Are you there, sir?"

"Put Detective Gurney on then, please."

"They're both out, sir. I believe you could reach them at four."

"I see. Are these local officers or are they from out of town?"

"Local. They've been with us for years. Would you like to speak to someone else?"

"No. Thanks anyway. I'll call back."

He went to the room and sat down heavily. It was true that for a space he had even doubted Iris. There had seemed no other possible explanation. When he told Iris the cops could hold his money and he might never see it again, he was only half serious. Just because money had disappeared in that Chicago case didn't mean anything. It was an extremely rare occurrence, and the police theft was still unproven. Yet, now . . . It was a fantastic, diabolical mystery. Poor frightened Iris. Naturally confused. And worried sick.

He didn't stop to call again. He drove to Sunset and followed it to her place, pushing all the way.

He rang the bell, and she opened the door instantly. Her eyes were red, her cheeks puffy. At sight of him her face crumpled. "Barry," she sobbed. "I'm so sorry."

She held the door wide, he stepped in and she closed it behind him. They embraced. Oddly, the drapes were drawn and a single lamp lit the room.

He was about to question her, but she took his hand and led him toward the kitchen. She moved silently and with slow steps, as though some irresistible compulsion had overtaken her will. In the doorway she paused and gazed at him blankly. He looked beyond her into the room.

Kieffer put the glass down on the kitchen table beside the bottle of bourbon. Holding the gun easily, looking faintly amused, he tilted back in his chair. Gurney's .38 was on the table, and his hand was merely resting upon it. The third man was leaning casually against the refrigerator, but his .45 was cocked and pointed carefully at Lunsford's chest. The shades were drawn and the room was dusky.

"Come in, come in," said Kieffer. "Have a drink. You're gonna need one. My Christ, but you've had a day, eh boy?"

## CHAPTER SIXTEEN

LUNSFORD TURNED TO Iris. She moistened her lips. She opened her mouth to speak, looked at the men and was silent.

"Go ahead," said Kieffer. "Tell 'im."

"They're not policemen at all," she began. "When they came last night, they said they were and I believed them. So I let them in." She spoke in a small flat voice. Softly, as though the men were in another room and might overhear. "They knew all about us—that we were engaged. They guessed that you had told me about the money. And—and because I thought they were police, I admitted it. I—I even told them how much and where it was."

She sighed. Her fingers played with each other nervously, sought the diamond engagement ring, began to rotate it.

"Then they forced me to make that call to you, telling you I had phoned the police and they were coming over. They left this—this other man—" her eyes drifted anxiously to the one leaning against the refrigerator, smirking—"they left him here to guard me."

"If you'd of got suspicious and called in to the station," Kieffer said proudly, "they'd of told you there sure was a Kieffer and Gurney but they'd gone out on assignment. We checked on those guys and used their names. You play this game for keeps, you don't miss any angles."

"You missed one, all right," said Lunsford, who was thoroughly shaken and wanted the small reassurance of hearing his own voice. "A California police car wouldn't have a chrome-plate calling card from Wilton Chevrolet, Jacksonville, Florida, on the rear deck."

The three men tossed glances at each other.

The bogus Kieffer nodded slowly. "That was a dumb boner," he said. "But it's gonna be the last."

"When you got away, they came right over here," said Iris quickly, with the first edge of defiance in her tone. "They knew you'd call. They said they'd find you sooner or later and kill you if I didn't get you here with that money. And—and they had a knife at my—at my . . ." She gazed down at her breasts and began to weep softly. Then she looked up. "Barry—oh, Barry! They just want the money. For God's sake, give it to them!"

"That's what we want," said Kieffer. "Just like the little lady said. That dough will buy you out of a mess of grief."

Lunsford put his arm around Iris. He stroked her head. "Don't you worry, baby," he said.

"Jesus Christ, those two are gonna make me blubber all over myself any second," said the one who was posing as Gurney.

"Shut up," said Kieffer. "Our boy is about to see the light. Play it cozy, though. Check if he's got a piece. And a couple of keys, maybe. Like bank keys."

Gurney crossed the room swiftly and stepped behind Lunsford. "Arms up," he said. Lunsford raised and felt the hands thump over him, searching his pockets, coming up with the keys to the deposit box. Gurney returned to the table and sat down, holding the keys up smugly, then tossing them to Kieffer.

"How about it, Lunsford?" The one by the refrigerator spoke for the first time. He was younger and shorter than the others, and wiry, with dark skin and deep circles under his eyes. He had a sharp nose, thin lips and mocking eyes. When he spoke, his eyes slid to Kieffer in an attitude of deference, as though he were signaling for permission. He was wearing slacks and a sport shirt. The phony cops had removed their coats and loosened their ties.

"How about it?" said the younger one again. "A trade. You get the girl and we get the dough."

"Otherwise?" asked Lunsford.

"There's no otherwise!" barked Kieffer, fingering the hammer of the .38. "We'll get it this way or that." He grinned. "How's the operation? Healing up, is it?"

"You should of been a surgeon, Chet," said the one with the .45.

"I dunno, Perry. Don't think so. I get nervous. I start with a little slice, about that big. Next thing, I forget myself, I got three inches of steel in a guy. Could be dangerous. No, I should of been a butcher."

Gurney laughed, a raw sound. Lunsford made note that Kieffer was called Chet, and the young one Perry.

"Now," said Chet. "We could take that same knife and we could operate on the girl friend, Iris. C'mere, Iris honey."

She looked at Lunsford, hesitating. Unreasonably, he felt a loss of manhood. There was nothing he could do.

"You heard him," snapped Gurney. "Move!"

Chet disparaged the order with a wave of his beefy hand. "Can it, Buck. She knows her master's voice. Now, c'mere, Iris honey."

Iris moved slowly across the room, then paused a few steps away.

"Closer," said Chet in a voice latent with sly undertone. As Iris moved, he handed his .38, butt first, to the one identified as Buck. As though there would now be need of a special alertness, Buck trained it and his own weapon purposefully on Lunsford, who said, "Leave her alone, Kieffer, or whatever your name is. I never said I wouldn't deal with you."

"We'll give you something to remember, case you think of changing your mind later," said Chet, reaching into his coat pocket, palming something to which he gave a back flip of his wrist. There was a click, and the long dagger blade of a switch knife pointed a shining steel finger at Iris.

"You take one step back, Iris honey," said Chet, "and this baby will snake out at you and cut you dead. You understand?"

Tearfully, Iris nodded.

He caught her wrist with his free hand and, reaching up, slashed the knife down the front of her blouse. The cloth parted neatly all the way, with a thin sound of tearing.

"You see," said Chet, as Iris whimpered and the other two eyed the exposure of bra with fascination. "Good steel. A razor. Now watch."

The knife sliced again. The bra parted cleanly. He yanked it away, and it dropped to the floor. Her breasts surged free, heaving whitely with the sobbing intake of her breath.

"Man!" said Perry.

"Papa, carve me some of that!" said Buck.

Lunsford tensed, leaning forward.

"Don't try it," said Buck.

"We could operate about here," mused Chet. "Like this." He cut a line downward between her breasts. A fingernail scratch and tear-drops of blood appeared as the knife descended.

"Don't!" she screamed in terror. Then anger flushed her cheeks.

"You filthy bastard," said Lunsford.

And at that moment Iris struck Chet across the face.

For seconds there was only the echo of the sound,

a taut immobility in the room. Chet stared at the point of the knife. His lip twitched, his eyes darkened and something foreign and grotesque shadowed his features. Watching, Lunsford saw neither quick punishment nor slow torture. He saw death.

Buck saw it, too. "No!" he shouted. "Save it, Chet. We're gonna need that one."

Chet took a deep, shuddering breath. It seemed as though the shout had awakened him. He gave Iris a shove that sent her sprawling to the floor.

"I'm gonna remember that," he said. "If you come outta this alive, depends on your boy friend. But either way, you'll pay, you bitch! We'll make a zombie outta you. Now take 'er in the other room, Perry. Cuff 'er to the bed and come out. We got business to talk with Lunsford, and I want his mind on it."

Perry hoisted her from the floor and took her away. As she passed Lunsford, he gave her arm a squeeze. She sent him a pitiful, pleading look, and a hardness came into him he hadn't known was there.

"I have a feeling," he said to Chet, "that before this is over, I'll kill you. That feeling just came to me. It's a new one. And you know something? I like it. I like it fine."

"Here I am," said Chet. "Why wait? Don't let a slug stop you. Just keep on comin' . . . No? A phony. No guts. Soft, like all the little creeps out there saving their pennies so we can take 'em away. All right, so it's my deal. We got the girl friend and you got the money. We want that money, Lunsford. Or the girl dies. Slowly. We'll mail 'er to you. Piece by piece. One day you'll get a hand with the ring still on the finger. The diamond you bought with our dough. Next day you'll get an arm. And then a foot and then a leg. And if that don't crack you, one day you'll get a head."

"You think we wouldn't kill the girl?" asked Buck. "Just the way he says—chunk by chunk."

Chet got the safety box keys out and held them in his hand. Perry came back into the room and took up his position by the refrigerator, the .45 stuck in his belt.

"Maybe we should send Perry down to the bank with him," said Buck. "If Perry don't show at the hideout on time, then we start slicing the cookie."

"Too risky," said Chet. "Lunsford gets in the bank, he tips the cops and maybe they can sweat Perry. No. We send this boy alone. He'll play. He knows the girl friend don't mean a thing to us and we'd finish her. Right, Lunsford?"

Lunsford was silent, saving his hate for action.

"Okay," said Chet. He tossed the keys, and Lunsford caught them. "You still got an hour before the banks close." He reached under the table and came up with Lunsford's brief case. He hurled it at Lunsford's feet. "You take the case and you fill it and you go back to your apartment. You'll find the phone behind the couch where we hid it. Cord's not even broken, just pulled loose from the terminals. You hook it up again. Any dope can do it, with a screwdriver. You wait for a call. Midnight on the button. You'll get orders. You obey down the line.

We get the money and we set the girl free. Until then, not a cop in this world could find us where we're goin'. So keep your mouth shut. We got a nose for cops. One smell and your cookie is finished. Now take that case and beat it."

Lunsford picked up the briefcase and walked to the door, and they followed. An idea was coming to him. As soon as he left, he would call the police before they could get away. Chet killed that immediately.

"Perry," he said. "Hike out with Lunsford to his car. Hold him there until we've got the prints wiped and the girl set to leave."

Lunsford turned to Chet. "I won't gamble with Iris' life," he said. "You'll get the money. All of it. On one condition."

"No conditions, wise guy," said Buck.

"Let 'im talk," said Chet.

"When you call at midnight, you put Iris on. Then you be ready to deliver her to me unharmed. And I mean untouched by any one of you apes. When I have her safe, you'll get the money. Not until. Not one goddam cent."

"Look who's givin orders," said Perry.

"No deal," said Buck. "We call all the turns."

Chet scratched his ear, studying Lunsford thoughtfully. "I can read this one good," he said. "The bastard ain't bluffing. He'd hold out. And you know, he's smart." He winked at Buck. "Okay, we deliver the girl first." He poked the barrel of the gun in Lunsford's cheek. "But you better have that dough, sonny. So you can get your hands on it in ten minutes. Or you and the dame will both be dead before morning. Now, get outta here!"

He went out with Perry behind him.

## CHAPTER SEVENTEEN

As soon as he drove away from the bank with the money, he began to watch again for a tail. Traffic was heavy on Wilshire, and it was difficult to spot any particular car. He turned off at Beverly Hills and took a residential street north toward Sunset. It was then that he saw the gray sedan. The two men behind the windshield were wearing sun glasses and hats. He couldn't make them out. He wheeled in another direction, and they followed. He swung back north again, and they were there. Well, he was expecting it. There was very little he wasn't expecting. He took the gun from his pocket and laid it on the seat. Then he gave a heavy foot to the accelerator.

That sent him rocketing ahead. He wanted to see if they were determined enough to give themselves away. They were. He tooled east on Sunset. He gave them time to get set not far behind him, then poured on the gas, praying for a police car to pick him up. If he knew anything at all, the cops would want to bag them both. Then the fun would start. And with any kind of luck . . .

But suddenly police cars were as scarce as taxis in the rain. And, just as soon as he hit the Strip, the tail got cautious and slowed. Now he had to crawl because traffic obstructed passing. The tail closed ground. He could turn a hundred corners and might not lose them.

Then he did see a police car. It was sitting at the curb near the traffic light at Fairfax. He pulled in behind it and waited. The gray sedan did the expected. It slid on by and swerved right at the corner. Lunsford pulled out again and went left. He made a series of turns and lost the tail. Round one.

At the motel on Olympic he hid the brief case and went out, locking the door. The phone booth was close enough so that he could watch the room.

He called the manager of the Seaview, Mr. Symon. He explained that there had been a small party at his place the night before. Some joker had yanked the phone out and had hidden it as a very unfunny gag. He had just learned that the instrument was supposed to be behind the sofa. Would Mr. Symon go up with his duplicate key and check? Mr. Symon would and did. The instrument was there, and the cord seemed undamaged. Now, would Mr. Symon please connect the wires to the terminals and wait there until he, Lunsford, called in to see if the phone was working? Mr. Symon would.

Lunsford delayed ten minutes, then dialed his

own number. Symon answered and that was that.

For a long time, then, he sat very still in the room. There was deep sadness in him. For Iris. To think that because he possessed this money, because of his greed, she might die. Or be tortured. Or, even at this moment, be raped . . . She was a lamb in a jungle. The thought of her loneliness and terror numbed his brain, convulsed his stomach.

He hated the money now. He wished they had it and he had Iris and it was over. If only it was that simple. A mere exchange. But no, it wasn't going to be that simple. Because her safety, and his, would end the minute the money changed hands. People who can talk and identify must be made very dead. Like the guards in the armored car. He wasn't fooled by promises. He understood the irony. The money would not buy freedom, but death. And yet to withhold the money past midnight would be death also. For Iris, at least, a slower, more violent death . . .

"We'll mail 'er to you, piece by piece . . ." And they would. They'd do it just that way. And he'd break. Oh God, how he'd break!

He had until midnight to think of something so subtle, so clever, they would be taken in. But what? He could neither attack nor defend until that call gave him a direction in which to move.

Midnight. Why midnight? Why not now? Or an hour from now? Why hadn't they said, We'll give you an hour for the round trip? Bring the money back here one minute late and she'll be dead. Naturally, because he could then return to Iris' apartment with the police. They needed time. Time to hide. They had planned to take the money from him when he left the bank. But, failing, they must have a much more elaborate scheme. And if it required until midnight, that would mean distance was involved. "Not a cop in the world could find us where we're goin'." So the hideout must be quite distant, and probably a place that was, to a degree, invulnerable and inaccessible.

Time was the one factor in his favor. But what next? Should he go to the police? What a comfort to have the local police, the FBI and God only knew how many other interested agencies behind him. It was a big case, the robbery of federal money, the killing of three guards. It would create a tremendous stir. The area would be crawling with cops, the earnest ones, the glory hunters, the men who just did their jobs. All kinds. Active. Running in all directions.

Great. But could so many men operate in secrecy? Enough to fool watchful eyes? Maybe. If these killers were amateurs or just small-time punks. But they had stolen close to a million from an armored car —an almost impossible feat. It took a kind of genius. And they had an uncanny knowledge of police operations. They would know. They would see, hear, smell, sense this swelling activity, this motion and preparation for their capture. And at that moment the money would become comparatively unimportant to them as set against their capture and execution. Didn't they still have six hundred forty thousand? A good part of it new money, perhaps. But it could be spent—in time. No, they would vanish at the first hint of police—and Iris with them. He couldn't risk it. Why, with so much organizing by so many, some reporter might even get hold of it. And then another and another, all nosing about the scene, thoughtlessly destroying the hope of contact.

No, the thing to do was to use the time to advantage. Try to uncover the hideout with what facts he knew. Hopeless, maybe. But, try, try! Then, and only then, would he summon help. He would start with a look at Iris' apartment. Just give him a single clue. Just one. But first he had to attend to the money.

He got the case from hiding and left the motel.

## CHAPTER EIGHTEEN

HE DROVE TO SANTA MONICA by way of Olympic. He stopped at a store and had the case wrapped with brown paper and string so that it had the look of an ordinary package. Then he parked the car and, slumped far down on the seat, taxied to the back entrance of the Miramar Hotel. He gave the package to the driver and watched him take it inside. In less than a minute, the cabby was back with the check, telling him, Yes, any time of the night he could retrieve the package. If the checkroom were closed, there would always be someone around with a key to unlock it.

As the cab returned him to his car, he removed a shoe. Unseen, he shoved the small metal check beneath the lining.

In twenty minutes he was at the door to Iris' apartment. He wasn't surprised to find it unlocked. He went in. The drapes were still drawn, and a single light was burning. The airless atmosphere was close, pungent with spent tobacco. The silence, insinuating her loss, was depressing.

He moved from room to room, studying everything minutely—floors, tables, chairs. The place was immaculate. Not a butt in a tray, a scrap of paper, a book of matches. Glasses in the kitchen cleaned and put away, the whisky bottle gone. There wouldn't be a print in the apartment that didn't belong to Iris. He knew it.

In the bedroom he opened the closet and stared at the rack of dresses, spying the one she had worn the night he had given her the ring. He fingered the skirt, rawness in his throat, anger throbbing his temples. He could beat the one called Chet until his face was a red mash or stick his own knife deep in his gut and watch him die with insane pleasure. He could stand them all against a wall and shoot them dead without ever once waking in the night, haunted by their bloodless faces. He was tortured by the need, so foreign and violent, to kill without remorse or pity. But cold logic, not emotion, was needed.

He left the bedroom, locked the outside door and sank into a chair. For long minutes he stared at the rug, groping for the fragment of an idea. He hurried down a dozen avenues of thought and found them all dead ends. He plucked the one senseless clue from his pocket—Vida's note. He read it again and again.

TROUBLE WITH L. MEET YOU AT THE SHORE.

V.

He could ride the entire shore, looking for a black Ford with a Florida plate. He could waste hours and never find it. Better to trace Vida's reasoning.

She had left the note for a C. Barnum. C could stand for Chet and probably did. Barnum was doubtless an alias, true names being dangerous in their game. But if Vida expected Chet and Chet alone to read the note, why was she so vague? Perhaps she wasn't vague at all. Maybe the word shore had a much more specific meaning. Like saying, Meet you at the park, the other person understanding exactly where in the park. Logical, but only discouraging. Try another tack. Suppose she had simply shortened a proper name. Meet you at the Park... Central Hotel. Meet you at the Shore...?

He got to the phone in a hurry and dialed information. An emergency—please make every effort. Was there anywhere along the near coast, say fifteen miles in either direction, a hotel, motel, restaurant or bar which contained the name Shore?

At first the girl was irritable over the task. But he kept placating, kept urging her on, warming her up, making himself human to her—and desperate. Until she finally found something. North of Malibu on the Pacific Coast Highway. A place called The Shore Club. The girl said she had heard of it, thought it was a restaurant or night club. She gave him the phone number and address.

He arrived in Malibu at dusk. Stalling for darkness, he stopped at a bar. He ordered a highball and drank it slowly. He found the wall phone and the chained Malibu directory on the way out. He looked in Classified.

### THE SHORE CLUB

*Specializing in seafood and your favorite mixed drink. Dancing and entertainment nitely except Monday. Motel accomodations.*

He found the place with difficulty. It was set well off the highway on a hill. It rambled low on the edge of a steep cliff overlooking the Pacific. But for the small neon sign at the dirt road entrance, he might have missed it. The road jogged him through a flat waste, sparsely treed, then curved to a parking area before a squat building. Off to the right, there was a scattering of dismal cottages.

The Ford was not in the parking area. Nor was it standing beside any of the cottages. He entered the main building.

The place was larger than he had imagined. It stepped part way down the side of the cliff, presenting a steep crow's-nest view of the ocean. The first level contained an office to the left and a dim bar to the right. An odd assortment of salty and Bohemian types conversed noisily in the gloom of the bar. The next level below was a lounge, with cloistered booths where drinks were served on candlelit tables.

On the lowest level a small dance floor in a long narrow room was surrounded by tables for dining.

It might once have been a place where even the elite of the movie colony had gathered. But now there was a look of aging wood in need of paint, and a damp briny smell clung about the rooms. The customers seemed no more than glorified beachcombers, beatniks and a few kids fresh from their teens seeking a retreat where darkness and tap beer could be bought for a small price.

Lunsford stepped into the office and asked the seedy man in the yachting cap behind the desk if there was a Vida Sattler registered in one of the cottages. No? Was there anyone by the name of Barnum? Yes, there was a Mrs. C. Barnum in Number Seven. Her husband? The lady was alone, thought occasionally her husband joined her upon his return from various "business trips" throughout the state. Mrs. B. had been at the cottage for more than a month. Off and on. When she wasn't visiting with "friends." Generally Mrs. B. arrived at The Shore Club for dinner every night about this time. If the gentleman would care to have a drink at the bar and wait...

Lunsford found Number Seven to be the last cottage in the group—and the most secluded. It was dark, door and windows locked, shades drawn. There was a rusting metal chair on the narrow excuse for a porch. He dropped into it and, clutching the .38 in his lap, waited.

She was forty minutes coming, the headlights of the car threatening his concealment in the darkness, so that he had to duck around the side of the cottage. When he heard her step on the porch, he came on cat feet behind her, catching her neck in the crook of his arm and squeezing off her scream.

He took the key from her hand, opened the door and fought her inside. He found the light switch and kicked the door with his foot. He released her, and she turned.

"You!" she gasped. She seemed almost relieved. "I thought it was..."

"Chet?"

"You get out of here before I..."

"Call the police?"

Rubbing her neck, she stared at him blankly.

"Why don't you call the police, Vida?"

She sat down with an air of sullen resignation.

"What you want with me?" she said.

"Where's Chet?"

"I don't know any Chet."

They were in a small sitting room. Beyond was a bedroom. It was empty. Watching her, he shoved the bathroom door open with his foot and found nothing. In her lap, Vida held a purse, a brown suede one.

"I'm glad to see you have more than one pocketbook," he said. "I was worried, Vida. I was afraid I wouldn't be able to find you and return the black one. Yes, I was worried. No, really I was. There was seven dollars and change. A lot of money for a hard-working girl. Here." He got seven dollars from his wallet and found change in his pocket. He tossed the bills and the coins to the floor at her feet. She didn't take her eyes from his face. "I'll have to bring the purse to you—in jail."

She moistened her lips. "You got nothing on me, so what do you want, anyway?"

"I'll take the other purse for a starter. The brown one there in your lap."

"There's nothing in it," she said. "Look, I'll show you."

She was so natural about it. Too natural. He leaped at her and caught her wrist. "Drop it, Vida! That's it. Now I'll just take this across the room where it won't tempt you."

He opened the purse and groped until he found the little .25 automatic. He checked it. The clip was full.

"You're getting in deeper every minute," he said, dropping the gun into his pocket. "Let's see what else I can find."

"You sound like a cop."

He looked up at her. "Listen, you slut. Before I get through with you, you'll wish I was a cop."

"What have I done to you?"

"That's what I'm finding out right now."

There was a roll of bills in the purse, ten twenties, four fifties and a five. Cosmetic junk, more money in a billfold. Also a Florida driver's license and three wadded pages torn from the true detective magazine. He read the license.

Her name was Vida Tiriolo, and she had a Jacksonville address.

"Tiriolo," he said. "That will be your real name.

Tiriolo," he repeated, musing. "Sounds familiar. Let's see now . . . Wasn't that the name of one of the guards who was killed in the armored car robbery?"

"What guard?" she said. "Listen, what robbery?"

"You don't get the part, Vida. You're a lousy actress." Excitedly he unfolded the pages, finding it quickly. He read aloud. ". . . and though they are long dead now, still crying in their graves for justice are Pete Quillen, Wally Trautman and Joe Tiriolo."

She shrugged. "There's more than one Tiriolo."

"I see. A coincidence. And another coincidence —you're from Jacksonville. Come off it, Vida!" He put the license in his pocket and tossed the bag at her. "Let me tell you something right now, Vida. So we understand each other. I'm made of different stuff than your killer playmates. I don't kill, and I don't torture women. Usually. But your hood pals are not men, and you're not a woman. You're all about as human to me as four snakes in a basket. And right now I can't think of anything I wouldn't do to you to find out what I want to know. So just try me. Just hold out on me and see what happens. Now—where's Chet, and what time are you meeting him?"

She was silent.

He advanced, grabbed her by the hair and gave her a sharp open hand across the face. Her mouth hung open with surprise and fear.

"Now, what time are you meeting Chet?"

"I—I don't know. He didn't say. He tells me nothing. He comes when he feels like it. Or when he needs me for something."

"Where will I find him right now?"

"I don't know."

He backhanded her across the other side of the face. She whimpered, and her eyes moistened.

"Cry," he said. "Sob and scream! See if it gets through to me. I'm just beginning with you. Where's Chet?"

"I don't know, I don't know. Honest, he doesn't tell me. He never trusts me."

He pulled her hair tighter. "Where are they hiding Iris Howland? Quick!"

"You could kill me," she said, sobbing. "And I wouldn't be able to tell you. I don't know."

"I might kill you," he said. "It wouldn't touch me to do it. Or I might just cripple you for life." He released her. "Get up. C'mon, c'mon! Up."

She obeyed. "What are you going to do to me?"

"Outside. Move!"

"No. No, I won't go."

"You will. Conscious or unconscious."

He got the .38 from his pocket and raised the butt over her head. She went out. He cut the light and followed her. In the darkness he pulled her along by the arm to the edge of the cliff. Together they looked down.

It was a straight drop to the small strip of beach below. A beach enclosed by giant rocks. Rocks pounded by the surf, half awash, spewing spray. To the right, where the drop was not so precipitous, wooden steps fell to the sand. Moonlight bathed the scene in a kind of cruel majesty.

"It's not far," he said. "About thirty feet at this point. I don't think it would kill you. The sand would break your fall. But you'd never walk again. You might be paralyzed for life. You sit in a wheel chair, staring out a window for an eternity of monotonous days, all the same. At night they have to lift you out of the chair and carry you to bed. You can't sleep and you cry in the darkness. You wish you were dead, but you're afraid to kill yourself. Everyone smiles and talks to you like a child. but no one wants you. Secretly they wish you would die and set them free of you. You're useless. A nuisance. You're alone.

"That's your future, Vida. If I don't get the truth from you in the next ten seconds."

He moved her nearer to the edge.

## CHAPTER NINETEEN

She studied his face in the moonlight, searching with a kind of animal instinct for truth or bluff.

"Would you really do it?"

"I'd really do it, Vida. I'm pushed too far. It's you or Iris, and that doesn't even involve a choice. Five more seconds." He grabbed her by the neck and began to exert forward pressure. He was so tormented that he didn't know himself if he would do it. She looked down, her eyes dilated, her face wooden with fear.

"All right. I'll tell you what I know."

He dropped his hand.

"I can't talk here. I'm too scared. Can we move back from the edge?"

"No."

"May I sit down?"

"No. Just talk."

"You'll be disappointed. There are things I don't know."

"I'd better not be disappointed. Where are they

hiding Iris? Tell me that. The rest can wait. C'mon. Spit it out!"

"I—" She turned toward him. "Look," she pleaded. "I wouldn't lie. I'm too scared to lie. That's one thing I don't know. Where they've got her. They didn't tell me. But I know most all of the rest of it."

He hesitated, reading her face, knowing she was telling the truth. "All right, I'll believe that for now. Start from the beginning. I want everything and I want it fast."

"Can I smoke? I'm so nervous."

"Later. Just talk."

She looked down to the sea. She shuddered, then began to speak in a monotone, hardly moving her lips.

"It's true. I was married to Joe Tiriolo. We didn't get along. I like excitement. I like to play. I like money. Lots of it. He didn't have any, and, if he took me out once a week, it was to a movie. I used to go out on my own. To see a girl friend. That's what I told him. But mostly I went out with men I met one place or another. He found out, and we separated.

"One of the men was a friend of Pete Quillen, the driver of that armored car. Not really a good friend, I guess. But they knew each other, and Peter brought him to a party at our place one night. He was a cop. He did traffic patrol out near the city line, south of town. He's the one you keep asking about—Chet. Chet McKowen."

"My God, a cop. A real cop?"

"Yes. He was. And we hit it off right away. He was crazy. He would do anything for kicks, for laughs. He wasn't married, and he was a real stud, too. Know what I mean? Not like Joe. Joe was a mope. A square. I fell down in a heap for Chet. I mean, just like I didn't have any will of my own. He got in my body and in my mind and I wasn't me any more. I was a kind of female Chet McKowen. Understand?"

"Yes. Hurry it up."

"I got to sneaking out with Chet at night once in a while. It was funny, because when I got caught, long later, it wasn't with Chet but someone else. Chet had the night duty that time. Anyway, Chet was like me, all for excitement. The kind that costs and costs. He was a police officer, yes. But just because he got a childish boot out of it and couldn't find anything else. He always needed money, and he took a bribe whenever he could get one from some tourist sucker passing through in too much of a hurry. When he was on night patrol there had to be two men, and his partner was this Buck—Willis Buckner. Willis—isn't that a name? And Chet and Buck would shake down the lovers parked in their cars. You know, catch them right while they were . . . and then give them a good scare, threaten to take them in, finally let him go—for a bribe. Once they even robbed a jewelry store. Right while they were on duty. Imagine! What nerve," she said proudly.

"I've got the picture. Who's the third one—this Perry?"

"Perry Jelk. He never was a cop. He was a runner for a bookie. Chet used to give him bets. He worships Chet. Just like me. And, like me, he's scared to death of him at the same time. Listen, have a heart, can't I sit down and have a cigarette?"

He looked at his watch, squinting in the moonlight. It was just after eight-thirty, and, unless he could pry some clue from her, there was nothing he could do until midnight.

"All right," he said. "Go ahead and sit. Smoke, too. But you lie to me and you'll be up and over."

"Have I lied once? I'm telling you everything. Every bit I know." She sat, got a cigarette from her purse and lighted it. She exhaled on a long sigh.

"Go on. The rest of it."

"I don't know how the thing got organized, what the three of them schemed among themselves. They never told me the details. But one night Chet asked me to pump Joe for all he was worth about the armored car setup. That was before we separated, of course. I asked him why, and he said, 'Never mind, it just might come in handy.' He had a whole list of questions he wanted me to ask. He said there was no hurry about it, that I should take my time with Joe so he wouldn't get suspicious. I had some questions of my own I wanted to ask Chet. But he never was the sort who would give you one word about what he was doing unless he felt like it. All he would say was, 'You do this for me, baby, and one day soon you and me will ride off together in a golden chariot. We'll be up to our eyeballs in hundred-dollar bills.'

"Of course I guessed, and was afraid and excited at the same time. I mean, I guessed it would be some sort of armored car robbery, but I didn't dream Joe himself would be involved or—or get killed. I wanted Chet and I wanted money, and it seemed a way. I asked questions, but I didn't want the answer, really. Just the results. Like everything just happens without you having to think about the messy part—just the fun.

"So I did it. I worked on Joe slowly—a few questions every now and then. It was easy. Because Joe never had anyone to talk to about his job—no one he could trust. And before, I had been bored with it. I just yawned in his face when he talked about guarding those silly trucks. But, just as soon as I showed a tiny bit of interest, he opened right up and told me everything I wanted to know. And a lot more. I passed it all on to Chet.

Then Joe and I separated, and I saw Chet all the time. On the quiet. Still secret. Not because he was afraid of Joe any more, if he ever was. But just because I was Joe's wife and it was better that we weren't ever connected. Chet and me. Now I know why it was so important.

"About a month went by, and Chet didn't even mention the armored car thing. I wouldn't have known anything was up at all. Except that he was with Buck and Perry a lot. They were always meeting in private. And Chet was jumpy, on edge with me. Buck had quit the force and had gone to work for his brother. It was just a dodge, and he quit a month after the robbery. Chet himself had resigned, and was working out the last week of his notice when it happened. He was supposed to go with some detective agency right here in L. A. Funny, because here you were with the . . . But, never mind—he actually did have the job lined up. It wasn't supposed to start for a while after he left the force, to give him time for a vacation. Ha!

"I had moved to a little apartment, and Chet was helping me out with the rent. He was so vague about everything. I had almost forgotten there was a plan cooking. Then, on that Thursday, in the evening, it was in all the papers that the truck was missing. Joe's truck. I guessed, but I didn't dare ask. Chet was grim and silent. Three days later they found it and—and the bodies. I didn't care about Joe any more, but I cried, I really did. I mean, I thought it was going to be just—just a holdup. Not —not anyone killed or anything. Nothing like that at all. Oh my God, no. I was practically hysterical.

"Chet said he didn't know anything about it, and I had damn well better keep my mouth shut. After all, wasn't I lucky to be rid of Joe? After that he was like someone else I never knew. I was scared of him all the time. But I couldn't leave him alone, either. He didn't tell me the truth for two weeks. Then he said Joe pulled a gun and tried to shoot it out and there wasn't any choice. He said they used the patrol car, and it was easy at first because he knew Joe and Pete Quillen, the driver, and Pete opened the door when he stopped them with some story about this Wally Trautman's wife being in an accident."

"All right, so then what happened?"

"Chet said I was just as involved as the rest, about like the driver of a getaway car; legally I was just as guilty as if I had killed those men myself. So I had better play along. Meantime, Chet was still in the department for a few more days, and he always knew what was going on. They weren't even close to guessing that he or the others were involved.

"So then, about a month later when it had sort of died down, Chet gave me his share of the money in one of those two-suiters and told me to drive south in this Ford he had paid for, go down the middle of the state and fly to the coast ahead of him, leaving from Fort Lauderdale, an airport that wasn't being watched, according to his information. He said, being a woman, I wouldn't have any trouble, no one would suspect me. And, anyway, he didn't dare carry the money with him. Even though his share was all in old bills. He had insisted on that because the whole plan was his in the first place."

"But," said Lunsford, "you ran into a roadblock, is that it?"

"Yes. At least I was almost on top of it before I realized. I got panicky. I made a U-turn and went back the other way. One of the cops saw me and chased me. I got out of sight for a moment at that railroad crossing. I hurled the case out the window, thinking to come right back for it. When the cop caught me I was doing ninety, and he took me right down to the police station. They asked a lot of questions, but they couldn't prove anything. I paid a fine, and they let me go. I came back and saw you parked there, looking at the tire. I didn't think much about it until I noticed that your shoes and trousers were covered with dirt. That was when I memorized your license number. When I came back, you had gone. And so had the money."

"That got you to my rooming house, but how did you trace out here?"

"I phoned Chet, and he flew to Miami to help me. The landlady said you had taken a plane to New York. But you weren't on any of the flight lists. So we checked Chicago and then L. A. We found your name. It was perfect. Because we were coming out here anyway. Chet took the job with the agency and quit in a week. The others joined us, and we all began to hunt you. Chet had to promise to trade a hundred thousand in old cash for new to get Buck and Perry to take any real interest.

"After that, it was just a matter of time. If you use your right name you can't go to a new city without giving yourself away. You join a library, you rent an apartment, you get credit in some department store, you get a new driver's license sooner or later, you sign up for utilities and you get a phone."

"My phone was unlisted."

"I know. We weren't able to get your phone number until after we found out where you lived. And that made it tough. But finally we figured you'd buy a new car since you sold the old one. You can't live in L. A. without a car. So, each one of us took a different make and we started calling the new car agencies from one end of town to the other. You bought the car in Hollywood. I found the dealer myself."

"Uh-huh. And where have you been living all this time?"

"Right here. Except when I stayed at the Miramar for a few days so I could make contact with you and get information for Chet."

"Sure, fine. And where were the others staying?"

"You're not gonna believe this. But I don't know. Chet would visit me here when he wanted to see me. Or he would call me. But once he knocked me down just for asking him where he was living. Like I told you, he never has trusted me completely."

"What about Iris?"

"The girl friend? I knew they were going to grab her to make you give up the money, but that's all I ever knew about it."

"I want more than that, Vida. You must have overheard something. You must have some clue to where they took her."

She shook her head. "No, because I seldom see the others from one week to the next. Chet is jealous, and he wanted to keep me separate from them." She laughed. "Hell, we couldn't all live together. So, when I see him he's alone. There's nothing to overhear. He tells me what he wants, no more. They've got the girl and..."

"And what?"

"Listen, I don't want it to happen. But it will. I know them. I know Chet. They'll kill her. Sooner or later, they'll kill her. She knows too much. Oh God, this killing will never end. You'll be next. And then —then me. Yes, maybe my turn will come, too." She began to cry. "I hate it, just the thought of these killings makes me sick. But I'm scared of Chet. I never crossed him. Until tonight when you—"

He caught her shoulders and shook her. "Snap out of it. You must know one little clue. Just one! Where do they eat? What bars do they go to? Where do they meet and when? C'mon, c'mon!"

"I'm sorry," she moaned. "I really am sorry for you. But I don't know one other thing. Except that we're all going to die. Soon. Who can tell? Maybe tonight."

"Yes, maybe tonight."

## CHAPTER TWENTY

HE TOOK HER to his car and held her there, waiting to see if Chet McKowen or someone, anyone, would show at Number Seven.

He told Vida that he had decided to take her along with him back to the apartment. He would hold her as a hostage. When the call came he would tell McKowen that if Iris was harmed, if she wasn't brought to him immediately, he would shoot Vida.

Vida laughed her harsh, bitter laugh. "Chet would say—go ahead and kill me. He only uses me, he doesn't love me. He never loved anyone in his life."

"Then why do you stay with him?"

"Because I have no one else any more. And because I'm afraid of him. Listen, what can the law do to me? Will I really die for my part?"

"No. He was bluffing you. You'll be an accessory before and after. If you had been along during the robbery, that would be different. As it is, you'll get a few years. I don't know how many."

"Are you going to take me in?"

"I don't know. You're a problem, Vida. If I take you to the police now, what good will it do me? It won't get Iris back. They'd buzz around and scare McKowen and his strong-arms off. Couple of ex-cops like McKowen and Buckner would spot a trap or a tail first thing."

For a long time they watched in silence. At eleven-fifteen McKowen had not appeared at The Shore Club or Number Seven. Lunsford got a section of clothesline from in back of one of the cottages and tied Vida securely to the bed in Number Seven. It wasn't necessary to gag her. All the near cottages were empty, and no one would hear if she cried out. Unless he could use her as a hostage, it was pointless to take her with him. She'd only be in the way.

He pulled up in front of the Seaview at twenty minutes before twelve. He saw no one about. Nor did he expect to. He took the elevator to five and entered his apartment. He checked the phone to see if it was still working. It was. He stripped and taped the smaller of the two guns, Vida's .25 automatic, to the inside of his thigh. He dressed again, leaving the .38 in his coat pocket.

He was more nervous than at any time since the whole thing had begun. He paced the floor, wringing his hands, taking great gulps of air. They were all going to die, Vida had said. Maybe tonight. One of those overdramatic statements made by people under the stress of emotion. And yet, he felt now that it was true. Maybe not all, but some of them were going to die tonight. The fact was whispered to him in the oppressive silence. Not Iris, not Iris! he prayed.

At three minutes before midnight, he went into the bedroom. He sat on the bed, staring at the phone. A harmless gadget like a phone looking suddenly lethal and cunning, as though it were conspiring to destroy Iris. It was warm in the room, but he shivered, colder than he had been the night he swam naked in a mountain lake.

Midnight and the phone stared back, squat and silent, treacherous. It rang at one minute after, and he plucked the receiver on the first trill of sound.

"Yes? This is Lunsford."

"You got the dough?" Chet McKowen. He had come to recognize the voice.

"It's ready."

"How long will it take to get it?"

"Let me speak to Iris."

"How long, creep!"

"Ten minutes, maybe less." He tried to sound in control.

"Go get it."

"You think I'm crazy!" he shouted. "Listen, you slimy sonofabitch, you knew the deal. You put her on the phone and then you find a way to deliver her to me. If I like the plan, I'll play. Not unless."

"You have the big sound again, eh boy? Nice and safe in the apartment, and you're a dictator. You watch it, sonny, or we'll slice up your cutie pie, huh?"

"You want the money or don't you?"

"We want it and we're gonna get it, bastard."

"Not unless I'm satisfied with the arrangement. C'mon, put her on, put her on!"

"I'll do better than that, creep. You wanna see 'er? Sure you do. Now you take a little walk for yourself. You hop down to apartment Three-C there in the building. And you knock on the door and you see what happens. Then you come back and five minutes from now you'll get another call. Be there!"

The line was dead.

It had the sound of a trick. Apartment Three-C was the empty one Vida had pretended to be renting. A horrible thought came to him. He raced out the door and down the stairs, pausing at the third floor exit to clutch the .38 in his fist.

There was no one in the corridor. All the doors stood closed, and there was the silence of sleep—the drones of the humdrum world, weary and unaware in their beds. He envied them all.

He remembered Three-C. It was toward the back of the building, and he knew why they must have picked it. It was at the end of a narrow hallway, around the corner from the main corridor. Thus it was somewhat isolated.

He found the door and tapped lightly with the barrel of the gun. The spy flap opened immediately. He saw an eye and part of a face.

"Barry!" In a hoarse whisper. It was Iris.

"Iris!" he said. "My God, my God!" He put the gun in his pocket.

"Be quiet," she said softly. "Please be quiet."

"Are you all right?" he said in a whisper.

"Yes . . . I—I'm all right." She sounded as though she might cry.

"Well, for God's sake, honey, open up and let me in."

"I can't."

"Why, why? Are you alone?"

"Yes, I'm alone, darling."

"Are you tied or anything?"

"No. Not now."

"Well, what's the—"

"The door is locked."

"How can that be? You should be able to open it from your side."

"I don't know what they did to the lock, but it won't open from inside."

"It's some kind of a trick," he said. "A stall. I can't figure it. It's insane. Have you been here all the time?"

"No. They had me in a big old house up past Malibu, right on the edge of a cliff above the ocean."

"Near The Shore Club?"

"I don't know, I don't know."

"But you're all right."

"Yes, they didn't harm me."

"Well, listen—don't you worry, honey. I'll get

Symon up here with a key, and if that doesn't work we'll break this door down."

"No," she said. "The one called Perry is around. I was tied and gagged, but he just now let me loose so we could talk. He threatened to kill you if I made a sound."

Lunsford reached into his pocket for the gun. At the same time he felt the presence behind him and turned.

"I'll take that, wise guy," said Perry Jelk.

Lunsford removed his hand, and Jelk, holding the .45, plucked the weapon from his pocket. "Upstairs again," he said. "Now we wait for the call. And you—keep your mouth shut," he said to Iris. "You don't make a peep. Or like we tole you, this boy is dead." He gave Lunsford a shove.

They went back upstairs.

## CHAPTER TWENTY-ONE

HE SAT BY the phone in the bedroom, and Perry Jelk stood over him, holding the .45 at his temple. Jelk's hand was steady and his eyes were bright with excitement. He had the look of a man who knew how beautifully the cards were stacked—in his favor.

The phone rang. Lunsford reached but Jelk struck his hand with the barrel of the gun and took up the receiver himself.

"Yeah? . . . Sure, who else? . . . Yeah. Right here, with the four-five up his nose. . . . Yup—he saw the merchandise. Had a piece on him, but I snatched it. . . . Yeah, wise guy. But he'll play now. So, you wanna talk? . . . Okay, in a while. See ya, Chet."

He gave the phone to Lunsford. "Talk fast and pretty, wise guy," he said.

"Hello."

"All right, where's the dough, Lunsford?"

"What's the arrangement?"

"We take a look at the dough. If it checks, I call Perry off. Then you wait exactly twenty minutes and you go down and get your cookie."

"I don't like it. You think you're dealing with a kid? What happens during that twenty minutes? Is that when you kill us?"

"What you want, sonny boy, a dozen eggs in your beer? You wanna free ride, no strings? Listen, bastard—we got no time to fool. Take it or leave it. You leave it, you're dead."

He didn't care about the money. It was of no importance at all to him—except as a protection for Iris.

"Have your goon bring her up here to my apartment," he said. "Then you tell him to leave. When he goes out, I'll write down the hiding place of the money and slip under the door. After that you can have your twenty minutes or two hours to run, if you want. I don't give a damn about you or the money now—just our necks. That's the deal—or I don't budge an inch, whatever you do."

Brave words, and he didn't know whether he could back them up if he was tortured. But it was the only chance and he would try. God almighty, how he would try to hold out!

Over the line, there was a silence that went on and on. Then—"What time you got, Lunsford?"

"Twenty-five after twelve."

"It checks. Okay. You're a real smart boy. But you lose, sweetheart. We got the ace. The big black one. One o'clock sharp you go down and look for your doll. You won't find even pieces of her. You look for Three-C, you won't find that either. You won't find nothing but a big goddam hole in the wall."

"I—I don't get it," he almost whispered.

"Sure you do. You got the crawls up the spine already." He chuckled. "A time job. Twenty sticks of dyna and a clock. Tick, tick, tick. I can almost hear it. But not the girl friend. She don't even know about it. One o'clock and she blows. Wham! And you could scrape her off the walls—if you could find a wall." He laughed.

"You're bluffing."

"Am I? You think about it. Think fast! And keep listening, pal."

The line went dead.

Trembling, he put the phone down. He looked up at Perry Jelk. Jelk was fingering the hammer of the .45 and smiling in an odd way, his eyes feverish with twisted joy.

"Clever, huh?" he said. "That Chet is a sneaky one, huh? Va va voom! Jesus Christ, I can just hear it. What a sound, huh? Va va voom!"

Lunsford wet his parched lips and looked at his watch. Twelve-twenty-seven. Thirty-three minutes. It could be a bluff. A fantastic coercion. Irresistible. And yet . . . The truth whispered itself. The man was psychotic. He was capable of just that kind of evil.

He looked again at Jelk, his face asking the question. Jelk only smiled and nodded and kept on nodding.

The phone rang.

"Grab it!" ordered Jelk.

"Yes?"

"What time you got there, Lunsford?"

He looked at his watch but didn't answer.

"I make it thirty-two minutes to go on the nose. Right?"

"You will let her out?" he said. "The minute I tell you?"

"No dice. After we see the cash—then she's out. Better hurry, lover."

"All right, all right!" he cried brokenly. "The Miramar Hotel. In the check room. The case is wrapped in a package, brown paper. The check is here, in my shoe."

"Okay, okay. Give the check to Perry, there. Then put him on."

He set the phone down and pulled off his shoe. He gave the check to Jelk, who took it with a sly smile and, holding the gun steady, put the receiver tightly to his ear.

"Got it, Chet," he said. For several seconds he listened, taking orders, making obedient sounds. Then he hung up. He took a white handkerchief and wrapped it around the metal disc, tying the ends together securely. Leveling the gun, he backed to the bedroom window. Every now and then he turned his head quickly, looked down and then back again. At last he opened the window and sent the handkerchief sailing down into the night. Then he closed the window.

"Now we wait," he said. "The loot better be there. All of it, pal. All of it!"

Five minutes sped past. Six. Eight. The phone rang. Jelk answered. He listened, grinning broadly. "Jesus, what a ball," he said, and hung up.

"So we finally cracked you, Lunsford, huh?"

"They got the money all right?"

"That's what the man said. You're a real square shooter, Lunsy boy. No hard feelings, huh? You think maybe we gave you a rib about the bomb?" He leaned back against the bureau, holding the big automatic easily, watching Lunsford's face with shrewd, narrow eyes. "Well, I'll tell you," he said confidentially. "A guy like Chet, he don't snow you. He plays for keeps. One o'clock, just like the man said, va va voom! And we're gonna let you live long enough to hear it, huh? Va va voom!" He laughed idiotically.

A strange calm had come to Lunsford. He had really known it all along. And now that it was fact, a small center of clarity—the eye of the hurricane—opened in his thinking.

"Iris, too?" he asked quietly. "You never intended to let her out?"

"For what?" Jelk looked incredulous. "To sing like Caruso? She goes at one—ladies first—va va—"

"Shut up!" said Lunsford. "Shut your goddam drooling mouth, you sadistic half-wit!"

Jelk straightened, his face coloring. He advanced, hunched forward.

"Who you calling half-wit? Listen, creep, you're dead. Another hour and you're a dead man. You want it sooner?"

"You haven't got the guts, you poor slob," said Lunsford. "Not unless you're told." The thing was raging in him, blind, uncontrolled. "What are you anyway, Jelk?"

"How come you know my name, huh!" he shouted.

"What're you anyway, Jelk? Why you dumb bastard, you're just an errand boy for those guys. You wouldn't dare go to the can unless they gave you the word. That's all you ever were to anyone all your life, right? Errand boy! You won't shoot me until you're ordered to. The only thing you ever shot off without help was your fat mouth. You won't even touch me unless mama tells you. So fly off, you limp-wrist fairy!"

He had been right in his estimate of Jelk. The guy had a wounded ego. A minor punk who secretly knew it and stole his glory, his self-esteem, from the truly tough and clever ones like McKowen and Buckner.

"I'm gonna blow that mouth out the back of your head!" screamed Jelk, stepping in, shoving the barrel in Lunsford's face.

"Now, now," said Lunsford mockingly. "Wait for the order, little boy. Those hard, tough men will slap your wrist."

He saw the gun barrel rise over his head, and as it came down he rolled and punched upward into Jelk's face. Jelk staggered back and Lunsford rushed him, kicking him in the groin, pounding his face when he doubled, hitting him rhythmically and continuously, feeling a knuckle-bone give, loving even the pain of it as Jelk sagged to the floor in gory-faced oblivion.

Lunsford grabbed the .45 and hurled himself into the living room and out the door. For a second he couldn't make up his mind if he should take the elevator or the stairs. Either one might be guarded. He decided to ride down to the second floor and sneak up one flight by the stairs. Especially since the elevator was already at five. He stepped in, pressed the button and descended.

He got off at two and raced up the stairs on quiet feet. He opened the exit door cautiously. The corridor was empty, a tomb of silence. On the balls of his feet he made his way over the carpet to the little branch hallway containing Three-C. He peered around the corner.

The sap in Buckner's hand came down viciously. He saw it and ducked, but not in time. It caught him a glancing blow across the right temple. The pain rocked his brain. He tried to hold onto consciousness with the violence of his will. All he could do was keep the gray-out from turning black. He felt himself slide down the wall, clutching with his fingernails, falling in a moaning heap.

He was turned over roughly, and there was the

feel of handcuffs enclosing his wrists behind his back. A gag was forced into his mouth, and, wretching unheard, he was drawn to his feet. He was half carried, half shoved down the hall.

He wondered how Buckner alone could have so much strength. But then in the elevator, as a fuller consciousness returned, he saw that Buckner was holding him by one arm and McKowen by the other. They were going up, not down, and in his bewildered state that puzzled him. Then the dizziness came again, his head dropped and consciousness diminished.

He had a vague awareness of the elevator descending. He was on the floor, looking up at two, three pairs of legs. Jelk was present now, glowering down at him from his good eye, the other swollen closed. He was mopping his bloody face with a red handkerchief, no, a washcloth, the maroon one from his bathroom.

His sight dimmed, the legs faded. He had a last dull impression that something dreadful was about to happen, that he had to stop it. Had to, had to! And then he swam downward through gray depths to darker shadows, into blackness. A void.

He arose from darkness with the sensation of being wedged in a mold, suffocating, while something flat and hard as a board stung his face again and again. He opened his eyes. He was sitting in the back seat of a parked car between Buckner and Jelk. McKowen was in front, leaning over the back of the seat and slapping him cruelly.

The slapping stopped, and McKowen said, "Goddam, Buck, goddam anyway. If you'd hit him any harder, he'd of missed all the fun." He laughed and was joined by Buckner. Jelk was sullen.

"You let me have him all to myself for just a couple minutes?" pleaded Jelk. "Okay, Chet? I get through, you could blow on him and he'd die."

"Shut up!" said Chet. "You damn near loused us up, you sonofabitch." He looked at his watch. "Three minutes to one. Hear that, Lunsford? Three minutes to go. Three minutes and your cookie blasts off. We got her tied and gagged right where she blows. Jesus, I'm gonna sit right here and watch your puss the whole time." He chuckled. "Christ, what a show!"

"He don't even know where he's at," said Buckner.

"Sure he does," said McKowen. "Anyway, we'll show 'im. Look there, Lunsford. Up ahead and to the right about half a block. That's it, the Seaview. Got it? Okay, now walk up three stories and you'll see a light. Can't miss it, it's the only one."

Lunsford was bent down and forward, holding his head against the brutal throbbing. He saw now that they were on a side street in back of the building, placed so there was an oblique distant view of the right wall. The wall was completely dark except for a single light, the palest glow behind a drawn shade.

The entire meaning broke upon him, and his

eyes were drawn to the light in a sick horror of fascination.

"One minute," said McKowen. His teeth gleamed in the darkness.

"McKowen," said Lunsford in a dead, sunken voice. "It's a joke, isn't it? Tell me it's a joke, McKowen." His voice rose. "For God's sake tell me it's a joke!"

"It's a joke," said McKowen. "Biggest goddam joke of my whole life. Twenty seconds."

Lunsford looked at the faces of the two beside him to read the lie. But what he read was awe, naked awe on their open-mouthed, wide-eyed, peering-upward faces.

He remembered the little gun then. Taped to the inside of his thigh. And he thought how at least McKowen would die in front of it, forgetting for a fleeting moment that the hands writhing in back of him were handcuffed.

"Five seconds," said McKowen. The other two were silent, not stirring a muscle beside him.

Lunsford began to pray aloud, a kind of gibberish he couldn't understand himself.

"Time!" said McKowen.

Almost on top of the word the tiny light blew out, and, as though a giant wind, tornadic in violence, had whirled and thrust itself from that third floor cubicle, the wall spewed outward and showered down in great fragments of flying cement. The sight came an instant before the sound, which rumbled and thundered to them in waves, street and car trembling together, the last echo that of debris showering the ground below.

Then, behind the exhale of smoke, a small flame kindled in the open mouth of wall, flared higher and gave an eerie light to the smoking interior. But in the socket of the wound, there could be seen nothing but the skeletal fragments of twisted timbers.

The silence then was unbelievable. As though the world for a mile around had stopped breathing. And in that silence, Lunsford moaned, "Aw no, now. Aw no, no, God. Not my Iris. Not Iris. Gone, just nothing. Aw no, it—it couldn't happen, it couldn't!" he screamed. "Iris," he sobbed. "Iris, aw, Iris." And, bending his head between his legs, he wept uncontrollably.

"It's a joke," said McKowen, backing the car furiously and swaying around. "Just a joke. My Christ, what a night, eh boys?"

## CHAPTER TWENTY-TWO

HE DIDN'T REMEMBER the ride. It was never real or clear. Just an impression of dim lights and shadow and coast line and the occasional flare of headlights bursting upon them, then dying suddenly. Shortly after they raced from the scene, slowing once lost in the traffic of the Pacific Coast Highway below the Seaview, he thought he heard sirens crying to the night, but he never was sure. It was all mixed in the throbbing hurt of his head and heart, the numbness of shock.

The others all were silent, as though in the aftermath they were too spent even to speak. And then the car rose to the summit of the hill north of Malibu, slid past The Shore Club and onward something like a mile, cutting left across the highway toward the sea, entering a dirt road between the wood posts of an open gate.

The house, perhaps a hundred yards from the highway, was two-story woodframe, a shabby eyesore of peeling brown in the headlights, though again he had only the vaguest impression of it.

They sat him on the floor and cuffed him, hands behind back, to the leg of an ancient upright piano. Shades drawn, they dumped the cash from the big brief case out upon a table. Adding to it crisp stacks of new money they brought from another room, McKowen redistributed the horde, giving to each a share of the old money, the count taking considerable time.

Finished, McKowen brought a ring from his pocket and held it up toward Lunsford.

"You know who wore this last?" He grinned wickedly. It was the ring Lunsford had given Iris. "Vida gets it," McKowen said and tucked it away again.

A new bottle of bourbon was broken open, and they drank from tumblers, offering him a glass in a strange contradiction of their natures. He nodded assent, thinking he might get free from the cuffs just long enough . . . But McKowen held the glass to his lips, and he just let the stuff drool down his chin to his shirt. He wanted no whisky; he wanted nothing but to kill.

Jelk, who seemed no longer interested in his personal revenge, was sent upstairs. He returned in something like fifteen minutes with two suitcases, then made another trip for two more. On top of the cases, McKowen set a shotgun, a .12 gauge pump type, first checking the load. All the faces were dark now, all business.

"We'll pick up Vida next," said McKowen. "Then we'll shove for the airport."

"How about the creep?" said Buckner.

McKowen picked up the shotgun again. "One blast and you could see through him," he said.

"You gonna do it here?" said Jelk.

"Naw," said McKowen. "We'll blow him off the cliff into the water. They'll be a long time finding him, if ever. Get 'im ready, Jelk."

While McKowen held the shotgun almost in Lunsford's face, Jelk got him free from the piano leg and relocked the cuffs.

"On your feet, Lunsford. Outside."

Well, maybe he would make a run for it and maybe he wouldn't. He had really died with Iris anyway. The long death. This would be the quicker, the less painful. He went to the door in front of them, wondering whether they would want him found with handcuffs that might be traced. If at the last moment they would loose him, then he could try to take McKowen with him . . .

"Outside, outside, Lunsford!"

He went down the steps slowly, the gun at his back. In the moonlight he moved forward to open ground, hearing them follow.

"Take the path, take the path to the left and—"

Light, harsh and blinding, three cones from as many directions, blending in a single focus, fell upon them. All of them stopped, rooted.

A husky voice, loudspeaker amplified, crowded the stillness.

"Hold there, you men! Police. Hands overhead. Drop the gun, you there!"

When Lunsford heard the shotgun blast, he knew enough not to run. He dropped and hugged the earth. Six feet away he saw McKowen cut nearly in half by the Thompson gun as he tried to pump another shell, saw Jelk fall dead on the first step of the house, Buckner just as he reached the door.

Even when the firing had stopped, he lay as in death, waiting.

"You Lunsford?" said the officer bending over him with the Thompson.

"That's right."

"Which one has the key to the cuffs, boy?"

"The one on the steps," he said.

The cop was freeing him as a dozen officers approached in the light. He stood up, rubbing his wrists, feeling only slight relief until behind the others he saw, running, scrambling toward him, Iris Howland. She had a wild, hungry look, and she fell into his arms sobbing. He was too numb and unbelieving, and all he could do was hold her and stroke her hair and say, "Oh my God, oh my God!" Over and over.

Symon, the landlord, came just behind her and explained.

"We saw the light, you see, me and the wife. We was drivin' home from a poker game, six of us play all the time, and we saw the light. And Martha says, 'That don't look like Three-C, I'll eat it.' And no one supposed to be in there at all. So we go up and I get the door open, and this lady is there tied up and we take 'er to our place and call the police. And no sooner have, than there's an explosion and it sounds like the whole building is coming down and—"

"I know," said Lunsford, reaching over Iris' shoulder and squeezing his arm. "I know."

"I love you, I love you," said Iris.

"Are you Lunsford?" said the paunchy man, the all but fat man in the gray suit who had puffed up alongside with another in dark blue, a dour balding man.

"Yes, sir. I'm Lunsford, all right."

"Like to have you come down to the station if you will, please sir. Got to write a report. Won't take long."

"Sure," said Lunsford. "Soon as we stop off at The Shore Club and pick up a prisoner for you. Are you a detective?"

"That's right, sir. Sergeant Kieffer, this here is Gurney."

"You're Kieffer!"

"Yes, sir."

Lunsford turned away, chuckling. Walking Iris toward the police cars, he began to laugh, tearfully, hysterically.

"What's so funny?" said Iris. "We're all nearly killed and what's so funny?"

"I love you," he said. "I love you and I love Symon and all policemen. Especially the fat ones. Like Sergeant Kieffer."

He began to laugh again and couldn't stop. He knew he was a little crazy and would go on being a little crazy. For a long time to come.

www.ingramcontent.com/pod-product-compliance
Ingram Content Group UK Ltd.
Pitfield, Milton Keynes, MK11 3LW, UK
UKHW041422180426
11947UKWH00007B/245